P9-CRU-880

The International Collection of

CLASSIC FAIRY TALES

This edition published 1998 by D. Sylvan Publishing, USA, by arrangement with Dami Editore.

Illustrations by Tony Wolf, Piero Cattaneo, Libico Maraja, and Severino Baraldi.
Translation, adaptation and layout for the English edition by Dami Editore, based on the original Italian edition.
ISBN: 1-890409-62-6
Printed in Italy by Officine Grafiche De Agostini, Novara.

The International Collection of

CLASSIC FAIRY TALES

D. Sylvan
Publishing

Contents

The Brothers Grimm - *page 6*

Hans Christian Andersen - *page 72*

Fairy Tales of England - *page 124*

Aesop's Fables - *page 162*

Carlo Collodi - *page 204*

Charles Perrault - *page 230*

Fairy Tales from the Far East - *page 270*

Fairy Tales from Russia - *page 330*

Fairy Tales of the BROTHERS GRIMM

The Brothers Grimm, Jacob and Wilhelm, were born in 1785 and 1786 respectively.

Grimm's Fairy Tales - It is difficult to underestimate the importance of the Brothers Grimm in the history of fairy tales: these German brothers created one of the most important collections ever.

The tale of "The Three Little Pigs" is among the many tales collected and retold by the Brothers Grimm.

The First Collection . . . was published in 1812, but additions and revisions were made until the late 1850s. In the end, *Grimm's Fairy Tales* contained over two hundred stories. It was the first real attempt to gather all of the oral tales known at the time. The Brothers Grimm were historians, however, and were very precise in writing down the tales, careful to respect their unique oral traditions.

An Inspiration - People were inspired to have access to these tales, which otherwise might have been lost or forgotten. In fact, the first translations into English were made in 1823. The clear presentation of these fairy tales made other uses possible: plays were written, beautiful dances were choreographed, movies were filmed, and elegant operas were staged, all based on fairy tales of one kind or another. Among the most well-known tales from the Grimm collections are: "Snow White," "Hansel and Gretel," "The Golden Goose," and "Rumpelstiltskin" (a German tale, of which British versions also exist).

In Germany in the 1800s writing was done with a quill and ink.

Below, a typical day in the years 1790 - 1810: Bavarian soldiers stand casually while a new steamboat chugs along the river. In the distance, the locomotive train transports goods, while people move from place to place using a horse-drawn carriage.

The Three Little Pigs

Once upon a time . . . there were three little pigs, who left their mother and father to see the world. All summer long, they roamed through the woods and over the plains, playing games and having fun. Wherever they went, they were given a warm welcome, but as summer drew to a close, they realized that folk were preparing for winter. Autumn came and it began to rain. The three little pigs started to feel they needed a real home. They talked about what to do, but each decided for himself. The laziest pig said he'd build a straw hut.
"It will only take a day," he said. The others disagreed.
"It's too fragile," they said, but he refused to listen.
Not quite so lazy, the second little pig went in search of planks of wood.
It took him two days to nail them together.
"That's not the way to build a house!" said the third little pig.
"It takes hard work to build a house that is strong enough to

stand up to wind, rain, and snow, and most of all, protect us from the wolf!" The days went by, and the wisest little pig's house took shape, brick by brick. From time to time, his brothers visited him, saying with a chuckle, "Why are you working so hard? Why don't you come and play?" "I shall finish my house first. It must be solid and sturdy. And then I'll come and play!" he said. "I shall not be foolish like you! For he who laughs last laughs best!" One day, the little pigs found the tracks of the big wolf. They rushed home in alarm. Along came the wolf, scowling fiercely at the laziest pig's straw hut.

"Come out!" ordered the wolf.
"I'd rather stay where I am!" replied the little pig in a tiny voice.
"I'll make you come out!" growled the wolf angrily. Puffing out his chest, he blew with all his might, right onto the house. And all the straw the silly pig had heaped against some thin poles fell down in the great blast.
The little pig slithered out from underneath the heap of straw, and dashed towards his brother's wooden house.

“Come back!” roared the wolf, trying to catch the pig as he ran into the wooden house. The other little pig greeted his brother, shaking like a leaf.
“I hope this house won’t fall down! Let’s lean against the door so he can’t break in!”
“Open up! Open up!” shouted the wolf, as he rained blows on the door.

Inside, the two brothers wept in fear and did their best to hold the door closed against the blows. Then the furious wolf drew in an enormous breath, and went . . . WHOOOOO! The wooden house collapsed like a house of cards.
Luckily, the wisest pig had been watching the scene from the window of his brick house, and he rapidly opened the door to his fleeing brothers.

And not a moment too soon, for the wolf was already hammering furiously on the door. This house was much more solid than the others. He blew once, he blew again, and then for a third time. But the house did not budge an inch. The wolf decided to try one of his tricks. He scrambled up a nearby ladder onto the roof to have a look at the chimney. However, the wisest little pig had an idea, and he quickly said to his brothers,
"Quick! Light the fire!"
The wolf was not sure if he should slide down the black hole. But the sound of the little pigs' voices below only made him feel hungrier. "I'm hungry! I'm going to try."
And he let himself drop. But his landing was much too hot!

The wolf landed right in the fire. The flames licked his hairy coat and his tail became a flaming torch. “Never again! Never again will I go down a chimney!” he squealed. Then he ran away as fast as he could. The three happy little pigs began to dance and sing. “Tra-la-la! Tra-la-la! The wicked black wolf will never come back!” From that terrible day on, the wisest little pig’s brothers set to work.

In less than no time, up went two new brick houses. The wolf did return once, but when he caught sight of the three chimneys, he remembered the terrible pain of a burnt tail, and he left for good. Now safe and happy, the wisest little pig called to his brothers, “No more work! Come on, let’s go and play!”

The Wolf and the Seven Kids

Once upon a time . . . a Mother Goat lived in a pretty little house with her seven kids. She often had to leave home to shop for

food. As she set off, she always warned her children, "Don't open the door to anyone. The wicked wolf is always lurking about. He has hairy, dark paws and a deep voice!" Mother Goat was right to warn her children. At that very moment, the wolf was lurking nearby, disguised as a peasant woman. He saw Mother Goat leave her house and tell a neighbor she was going to market. "Good!" said the wolf.

"I'll just drop by and gobble up a few kids for lunch."
He waited until Mother Goat was well out of sight. Then, removing his awkward disguise, he sneaked up to the goats' door.
"Open the door. It's Mother, back from the market!" he growled.
When the kids heard the deep voice, they remembered their mother's warning.
"We know who you are. Our mother has a sweet, gentle voice, not a deep, gruff one like yours, Wolf!"
The wolf banged furiously on the door, but the kids kept it tightly locked.
Then the wolf had an idea. He dashed to the baker's and got a cake dripping with honey to sweeten his voice. He gobbled down the cake and rushed back to the goats' house.

"Open the door, it's Mother!" called the wolf in a high voice.
It did sound a little sweeter.
The kids were about to unlock the door, when the little black kid, who was the smartest of all, stopped them.
"Show us your foot, Mother!" called the little black kid.
The wolf held up his hairy, dark paw to the window.
"Go away, wicked wolf! Our mother doesn't have hairy, dark paws," cried the kids.
Foiled again! But the wolf was not one to give up, especially when his tummy was empty.
He ran to the flour mill, dipped his paws in a sack of flour, and hurried back to the kids' house.
"Open the door, it's Mother!" he called once more.
"Show us your foot!" called the wary kids through the keyhole.
The wily wolf lifted a white paw to the window and the kids, now feeling safe, threw open the door.

What a shock they got! With a growl the wolf leaped into the house. The kids scattered in terror. One dived under the table, another crawled under the bed.
Alas, one by one the wolf dragged them out and gobbled them in a single gulp — all except the little black kid, who hid inside the grandfather clock.

Mother Goat walked anxiously back from the market.
As she came up the path to her house, she saw the open door.
"Oh dear, oh dear!" she cried.
She felt something terrible had happened. As soon as she stepped inside, she knew the worst. The wicked wolf had gobbled up all her children.

Mother Goat dropped into a chair, sobbing bitterly. But as she wept, the door of the grandfather clock swung open.
"Mother, mother!" cried the little black kid. "It was terrible!

The wolf tricked us into opening the door. I hid in the clock. I could hear him growling and crashing about the house, and I'm afraid he's eaten all my brothers!"
Mother Goat hugged her little kid. Then, taking him by the hoof, she hurried out into the garden, hoping that some of the kids might have escaped. From under a tree came the sound of snoring. It was the wolf, sound asleep after gulping down six little kids whole. From his stomach came squeaking sounds.
"Quick!" said Mother Goat. "Run and fetch a needle and thread and a pair of scissors."
Mother Goat swiftly slit open the wolf's stomach, and one by one the six little brothers popped out.
"Hurry and get me a pile of stones," whispered Mother Goat to her kids. Quietly as mice, they collected a big pile of stones.

Mother Goat slipped them into the wolf's stomach and sewed it up. When the wolf awoke, he felt a raging thirst. He dragged himself to the river's edge, complaining about his heavy tummy. "Argh!" the wolf grunted, leaning over to drink. But the weight of the stones tipped him into the water, and he sank to the bottom. Mother Goat and her kids watched from the bushes. How thankful they were! Never again would they fear the big, bad wolf!

The Adventures of Tom Thumb

Once upon a time . . . there was a giant who had a quarrel with a wizard. The giant told the wizard, "I could crush you under my thumb if I wanted to! Now, get out of my sight!"

The wizard hurried away, but from a safe distance, he cast a terrible spell: "Abracadabra! May the son your wife will shortly give you never grow any taller than my own thumb!"

After Tom Thumb was born, his parents could never find him, for they could barely see him. Tom Thumb preferred being with the little creatures in the garden than with his own parents. He rode piggyback on the snail and danced with the ladybugs. Tiny as he was, he had great fun in the world of little things.

But one unlucky day, he decided to visit his friend the frog.

He had just scrambled onto a leaf when a large pike swallowed him up. A little later, the fish was caught by one of the king's fishermen, and before long, found itself under the cook's knife in the royal kitchens. To the surprise of everyone, out of the fish's stomach popped Tom Thumb!

"What am I to do with this tiny lad?" said the cook to himself. Then he had an idea. "He can be a royal pageboy! He's so tiny, I can pop him into the castle cake I am making. When he marches across the bridge, sounding the trumpet, everyone will gasp in wonder!" Sure enough, the king and his guests clapped excitedly at the cook's skill. Tom Thumb became a pageboy, enjoying all the honors of his post.

He had a white mouse for a mount, a gold pin for a sword, and he was allowed to eat the king's food. In exchange, he marched up and down the table at banquets, amusing the guests with his trumpet.

But Tom Thumb didn't know . . .

. . . that he had made an enemy. The cat which, until Tom's arrival, had been the king's pet, was now forgotten. Wanting to get its revenge, it tried to attack Tom in the garden. When Tom saw the cat, he whipped out his gold pin and cried to his white mouse, "Charge! Charge!" Jabbed by the tiny sword, the cat turned and fled. The cat decided to try

something else.
Pretending to bump into the king as he walked down the staircase, the cat softly meowed, "Sire! Be on your guard! Tom Thumb is planning to poison you. I saw him picking some wild mushrooms in the garden the other day and saying something about cooking you an omelette."
The king sent for Tom Thumb and had him searched.
The mushrooms were found under the mouse's saddle cloth, where the cat had hidden them.

Tom Thumb was so amazed, he was at a loss for words. The king, without further ado, had him thrown into prison. And since he was so tiny, they locked him up in a clock. The hours passed and the days, too. Tom's only pastime was swinging back and forth on the pendulum. One night, a big moth came fluttering into the room. "Let me out!" cried Tom Thumb, tapping on the glass. The moth took pity on Tom Thumb and released him.

"I'll take you to the Butterfly Kingdom, where everyone is tiny like you. They'll take care of you there!" And that is what happened. To this day, if you visit the Butterfly Kingdom, you can see the monument that Tom Thumb built after his amazing adventure.

RUMPELSTILTSKIN

Once upon a time . . . there was a miller who everyone knew was very boastful. He told everyone that his mill was the largest, his house the cleanest, and his flour the whitest. His big words reached the king, and one day when the king was passing by he decided he wanted to meet this miller. The miller introduced his daughter to the king, and could not resist telling yet another story.

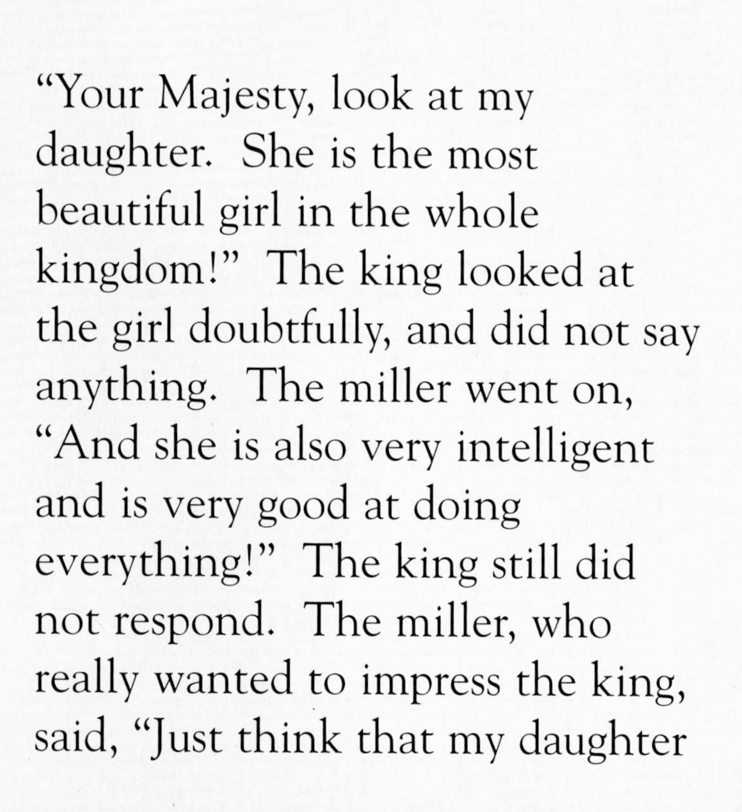

"Your Majesty, look at my daughter. She is the most beautiful girl in the whole kingdom!" The king looked at the girl doubtfully, and did not say anything. The miller went on, "And she is also very intelligent and is very good at doing everything!" The king still did not respond. The miller, who really wanted to impress the king, said, "Just think that my daughter

can spin straw and turn it into gold!" The king by then had had enough and said, "Very well, we will put her immediately to the test! If she can turn straw into gold she will be paid very well; if not, she will be put to death!" And he ordered his guards to take the girl to the castle.

The king closed the girl in a room with a pile of straw and gave her his orders: "Turn all of this straw into gold by tomorrow morning!" Left all alone the poor girl burst out crying. "In what mess has my father gotten me now?" she said through her sobs, when suddenly, out of nowhere there appeared a little gnome all dressed in red. He had a long white beard and he said to her, "If I help you turn all of this straw into gold, what will you give me in return?" The girl showed him a beautiful heart-shaped locket hanging around her neck and said, "I can give you this — it is the most precious item I own." The gnome accepted and the next morning the girl, who had slept fitfully during the night,

woke up to find that the little man had kept his promise. The king, on the other hand, who was certain that his order could not be fulfilled, opened the door of her cell and was ready to punish the girl. He stopped in his tracks when he saw on the table in front of him six spools of golden thread all lined up. Very pleased with this, the king decided to take advantage of the situation. "You have been very good, but I will send you more straw because I need more golden thread!"

The girl could not explain about the gnome, and she was more desperate than before. But that night, the gnome appeared again. "What will you give me if I help you this time?" he asked the girl. "The only thing I have left is this antique ring. Please, take it and help me again, otherwise my destiny is fated!" And once again, everything went just as the night before. The next morning the king

happily counted the golden spools into which the straw had been transformed. The girl also looked much prettier to him than she had before. He looked at her for a long time, and then he had an idea. "You will spin straw for me one last time, and if you can once again turn it into gold, I will marry you!" the king said to the girl. But the girl was very worried. "If the gnome comes back tonight, I have nothing left to offer him in return for his help. How will I be able to resolve this situation?" Desperate, the poor girl cried all night until in the dark of night the gnome arrived. "I am back once again to help you. But what will you give me this time?" In tears the girl responded, "Unfortunately I have nothing left to give you!" Smiling, the gnome looked at her and said, "I have found out that the king will marry you. When you are the queen, I will come and take your first child in exchange for helping you now." Without much thought the girl accepted and once again, the promise was fulfilled by morning. The king, who had become very rich with all of the gold,

assigned an apartment in one wing of the castle to the girl, and began the preparations for the wedding. The girl made the king promise that once she was married, she would never have to spin straw into gold again. The king granted her wish, and the marriage was celebrated.

The miller was very, very happy as one could imagine, and despite

everything, the marriage went quite well. The king and queen were very happy, even more so when a nice baby boy was born. By now the queen had forgotten her past misadventures until one horrible day when suddenly the gnome reappeared.

"I have come to take your son. Remember our agreement?" he said.

"No! No! I will give you all of my jewels in exchange! Ask me for anything, but I beg you, do not take away my son!" sobbed the queen. The gnome, however, seemed to have made up his mind. But he was moved by the queen's tears, and so he said, "All right, I will give you one last chance. If you can guess my name you can keep your son. But remember, you only have three days in which to guess, and you know what magical spells I am capable of!" And having said this the gnome disappeared. This time the queen ran to the king and told him the whole story. All of the wise men of the kingdom were called to the court, and they consulted their books to find the name of the gnome. Unfortunately, none of their manuscripts mentioned a gnome with a long white beard, dressed in red. Two days had already gone by when one of the king's messengers told of something strange he had seen.

As he was crossing the wood, he saw an old man dressed in red dancing around a flame, singing, "Tonight the child I am sure to claim, for none can guess Rumpelstiltskin's name!"
The third day arrived. The gnome suddenly appeared, and as soon as she saw him, the queen said, "Rumpelstiltskin!"
And a bolt of lightning struck the gnome and he disappeared in a cloud of smoke. The queen ran happily to embrace her child and said, "You are safe! No one will ever be able to take you away!"

Snow White and the Seven Dwarfs

Once upon a time . . . in a great castle, lived a very pretty little girl with blue eyes and long black hair. Her skin was delicate and fair, and so she was called Snow White. She had a stepmother who was also very beautiful, but she was a wicked and jealous woman. Every day, the stepmother would ask her magic mirror:
"Mirror, mirror on the wall, who is the loveliest lady in the land?" The reply was always,
"You are, your Majesty," until the dreadful day when she heard it say,
"Snow White is the loveliest in the land."
Furious and wild with jealousy, she decided to find a way to get rid of Snow White. Calling one of her servants, she ordered him to take Snow White into the forest and put her to death. The servant agreed and he led the little girl away. However, when they came to the forest, the man took pity on Snow White and, leaving her sitting beside a tree, he mumbled an excuse and ran off.
Night came and Snow White, left alone in the dark forest, began to cry bitterly.
She thought she could feel terrible eyes spying on her, and she heard strange sounds that made her heart thump.

At last, overcome by tiredness, she fell asleep curled up under a tree. Dawn woke the forest to the sound of the birds, and Snow White too, awoke. As she tried to find out where she was, she came upon a path. She walked along it, until she came to a clearing. There stood a strange cottage, with a tiny door, tiny windows, and a tiny chimney. Snow White pushed the door open.
"I wonder who lives here?" she said to herself. "There must be seven of them; the table is laid for seven people." Upstairs was a bedroom with seven little beds. As she went back to the kitchen, Snow White had an idea. "I'll make them something good to eat."
Towards dusk, seven tiny men marched homewards singing.

When they opened the door, they were surprised to find a bowl of hot soup on the table, and the whole house so clean that it sparkled. Upstairs was Snow White, fast asleep on the bed.

The chief dwarf prodded her gently.
"Who are you?" he asked. Snow White told them her sad story, and tears came to the dwarfs' eyes. Then one of them said, "Stay here with us!"
"Hurrah! Hurrah!" they cheered, dancing joyfully around the little girl. The dwarfs said to Snow White, "You can live here and tend to the house while we are down in the mine.

We love you and we'll take care of you!" Snow White gratefully accepted. The next morning, as the dwarfs set off for work, they warned Snow White not to open the door to strangers.
Meanwhile, the servant had returned to the castle, with the heart of a deer. He gave it to the cruel stepmother, telling her it belonged to Snow White. Pleased, the stepmother turned again to the magic mirror. It responded,
"The loveliest in the land is still Snow White, who lives in the seven dwarfs' cottage, down in the forest."
"She must die!" she screamed, wild with rage. Disguising herself as an old peasant woman, she put a poisoned apple with the others in her basket. Then, taking the quickest way through the forest, she arrived at the cottage just as Snow White stood waving goodbye to the seven dwarfs on their way to the mine.

Snow White was in the kitchen when she heard a sound at the door.
"Who is there?" she called.
"I'm an old peasant woman selling apples," came the reply.
"I don't need any apples, thank you," she replied.
"But they are beautiful apples and ever so juicy!" said the voice from outside the door.
"I'm not supposed to open the door to anyone," said the little girl.
"And quite right too! Good girl! And as a reward for being good, I'm going to make you a gift of one of my apples!" Without thinking, Snow White opened the door to take the apple.
"There! Now isn't that a nice apple?" Snow White bit into the fruit, and as she did, fell to the ground in a faint. The wicked stepmother hurried off. But as she ran across the swamp, she tripped and fell into the quicksand. No one heard her cries for help, and she disappeared without a trace.

Meanwhile, the dwarfs came out of the mine to find the sky had grown dark. Gray clouds covered every corner of the sky. Worried about Snow White, the dwarfs ran as quickly as they could down the mountain.

At the cottage they found Snow White, lying still and lifeless, the poisoned apple by her side. They tried to revive her, but it was no use. They wept and wept for a long time.

Then they laid her on a bed of rose petals, carried her into the forest and put her in a crystal coffin. Each day they laid a flower there. Then one evening, they discovered a young Prince admiring Snow White's lovely face. "She's so lovely . . . I'd love to kiss her!" He did, and as though by magic, the Prince's kiss broke the spell. And she came back to life! The Prince asked Snow White to marry him, and the dwarfs had to say goodbye.

From that day on, Snow White lived happily in a great castle. But from time to time, she came back to the little cottage to visit the seven dwarfs.

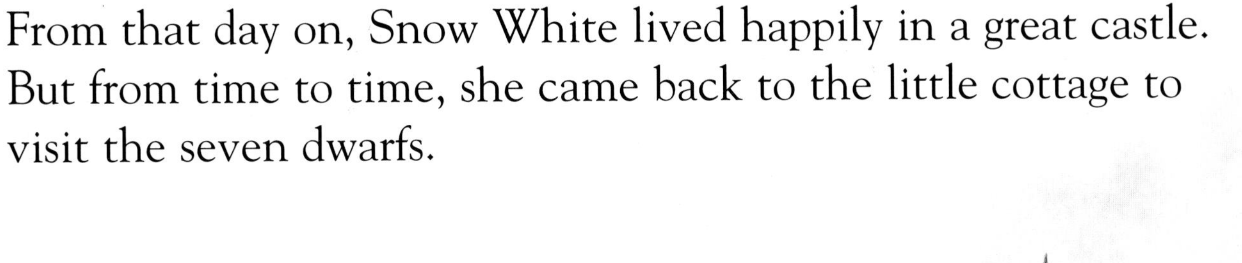

The Elves and the Shoemaker

Once upon a time . . . there lived a shoemaker. As he became old, he became poorer, for he couldn't work as well. One night, he went to bed, leaving a pair of shoes half done. To his great surprise, the next morning when he came into the workshop, the shoes were finished! During the day, he set out the tools and leather needed for a pair of shoes for a rich customer. "Tomorrow, when I'm feeling stronger, I will begin work," he thought. But the next morning, the shoemaker found a beautifully sewn pair of shoes. The customer was

delighted and paid the shoemaker twice the price. The shoemaker was confused, but that night he left out more leather. The next morning, there was another perfect pair of shoes. They sold at an even higher price than the previous pair. After this, the shoemaker left out leather and tools every night. Every morning, he found a new pair of shoes. Soon he was able to save a good sum of money. The shoemaker's wife became suspicious. "Who do you suppose it can be?" asked the shoemaker.

"We'll hide in your workshop and find out," suggested the wife. When all appeared quiet in the workshop, the man and his wife saw two elves tiptoe in. They set to work on a new pair of shoes, using the leather that the shoemaker had left out. How their needles and hammers flew! No wonder the shoes were so fine! It was winter, and the elves were clothed in rags. They shivered as they worked. "They must be very cold," the shoemaker's wife whispered. "Tomorrow I will make them two thick wool jackets. That way, perhaps, instead of one pair of shoes, they'll make two!" The following night, the elves found two elegant red jackets with gold buttons. They put them on and began to dance. "We'll never be cold again!" they chanted. "Let's get to work now," suggested one. "Work?" said the other. "What for? With two jackets like these, we're rich. We'll never have to work again." And with that, the two elves danced out of the shop; they were never seen again, but the shoemaker prospered from that day forth.

The Golden Goose

Once upon a time . . . there lived a woodcutter's son named Thaddeus, a dreamy, foolish-looking lad, but kindhearted. One day, his father sent him to a distant wood to chop down trees. What hard work it was! Thaddeus couldn't remember ever having so much trouble. At last, tired out, he sat down to eat. Suddenly a little old man with a white beard popped out from behind a bush. "Please, young sir, won't you give me a bite to eat?" asked the old man.

Thaddeus invited him to share his bread and cheese. The old man ate his portion hungrily, saying that the young woodcutter was the first to show him kindness.

"As a reward, I'll tell you a secret. If you cut down that tree in the middle of the wood, all the others will fall. Be sure to look in its roots!" And with that, the old man vanished. Thaddeus was not one to bother his head with questions. He did as he was told. In a twinkling his work was done. There, among the roots, sat a Golden Goose.

"My!" exclaimed Thaddeus, surprised for once in his life.

He tucked the Golden Goose under his arm and set off, but lost his way among the fallen trees.

It was dark by the time he reached a village and found a tavern. The innkeeper's daughter brought him a bowl of soup.

"A sip for me and a sip for you," said Thaddeus, sharing his soup with the Golden Goose.

The girl was amazed and asked why he was so kind to his goose.

"It's a magic goose," said Thaddeus proudly. "Give me a room with a good lock; I don't want to be robbed."

The girl told her two sisters about the Golden Goose. Later, the three tiptoed to Thaddeus' door and opened it with a master key.

The first sister tried to grab one of the Golden Goose's tail feathers, but her hand stuck fast. The others tried to pull her free, and found themselves stuck too! The next morning, Thaddeus awoke to find the three sisters sitting on the floor beside the goose, looking very uncomfortable. "Help us. We're stuck to your goose!" wailed the sisters. "I can't help that. My goose and I are leaving. You'll just have to come along," said Thaddeus.

The innkeeper saw Thaddeus going out the door with his three daughters. Angrily, he grabbed the last one — and became stuck! His wife ran after them, only to find herself stuck too. Before long the village pastor, the baker, and a passing soldier had joined the parade. Thaddeus walked along paying no attention to their shouting. The village people came to their doors and windows. Soon, a laughing crowd had gathered.

Near the village stood a king's castle. His only daughter was pining away and no doctor could cure her sadness. The king had sworn that any man who made the princess laugh would have her hand in marriage. The princess had chosen that morning to drive to the village square. Hearing the laughter, she looked out of the carriage window. There was Thaddeus, solemnly marching along with his goose and his strange parade.

The princess burst into peals of laughter. She stepped down from the carriage and the next instant, she had joined the parade, still laughing. Alarmed, her coachman set off for the castle, and Thaddeus followed along dreamily. The king was overjoyed.

He told the woodcutter of his promise. Kindhearted Thaddeus let go of the goose and took the princess' hand. The Golden Goose disappeared with a squawk and a flapping of wings, and at last everyone came unstuck. Thaddeus and the princess were married the next day. The Golden Goose had worked its magic, bringing fortune and happiness to the young woodcutter and his bride.

HANSEL AND GRETEL

Once upon a time . . . a poor woodcutter lived in a tiny cottage in the forest with his two children, Hansel and Gretel. Their mother had died, and the woodcutter's second wife often ill-treated the children. She was forever nagging the woodcutter.
"There isn't enough food for us all. We must get rid of the two brats!" declared the stepmother. She kept pestering her husband to abandon his children in the forest.

“Take them miles from home, so they’ll never find their way back. Maybe someone else will take them in.” The unhappy woodcutter didn’t know what to do.

Hansel comforted his sister. “Don’t worry, Gretel. If they leave us in the forest, we’ll find our way home.” He slipped out of the house and filled his pockets with little white pebbles, then went back to bed.

All night long the woodcutter’s wife nagged at her husband. At last, as the sun was rising, he led Hansel and Gretel into the forest.

Hansel secretly dropped the little white pebbles on the mossy green ground. All too soon, however, the woodcutter plucked up the

courage to desert them. He mumbled an excuse and was gone. Night fell. Gretel began to sob bitterly. Hansel felt scared, but tried to hide his feelings. "Be brave and trust me! I'll take you home, even if Father doesn't come back!" Luckily the moon was full that night. Hansel waited until its light shone through the trees. "Now give me your hand!" he said to Gretel. "We'll get home safely, you'll see!" The tiny white pebbles gleamed in the moonlight, and the children found their way home. They crept in through a half-opened window without waking their parents, and slipped into bed. The next day, when their stepmother discovered that Hansel and Gretel had returned, she flew into a rage. "Why didn't you do as I told you!" she shrieked at her husband.

The weak woodcutter was torn between shame and the fear of disobeying his cruel wife, who kept Hansel and Gretel under lock and key all day. They had nothing to eat but a crust of bread. All night, the husband and wife quarreled, but when dawn came the woodcutter once again led the children into the forest.

Hansel, however, had not eaten his bread. As he walked through the trees, he left a trail of crumbs behind. But the little boy had forgotten about the hungry birds. They flew along the trail, and in no time had eaten all the crumbs.

Again, the woodcutter left the children with an excuse.

"I've made a trail, like last time!" Hansel whispered to Gretel.

Alas, when night fell, they saw to their horror that all the crumbs had completely disappeared.

"I'm frightened!" wept Gretel bitterly. "I'm cold and hungry and I want to go home."

"Don't be afraid. I'm here to look after you!" said Hansel,

but he shivered at the deep shadows and glinting eyes in the darkness. All night the two children huddled together for warmth at the foot of a large tree. When dawn broke, they wandered about the forest looking for a path. Hope soon faded. They were well and truly lost. On and on they walked, until suddenly they came upon a curious cottage in the middle of a glade.
They drew closer to the little house.

"Why, this is chocolate!" gasped Hansel as he broke a lump of plaster from the wall.
"And this is icing!" exclaimed Gretel, putting another piece of wall in her mouth. Starving but delighted, the children began to eat pieces of candy broken off the cottage.
"Isn't this delicious?" said Gretel with her mouth full.
"We'll stay here," Hansel declared.
They were just about to try a piece of the biscuit door when it swung quietly open. An old woman with a crafty gleam in her eye peered out at them.
"Well, well! Aren't you the sweet-toothed little darlings! Come in, come in! You've nothing to fear," cackled the crone, opening the door wider.
No sooner were they inside than the witch — for it was indeed a witch — grabbed Hansel and squeezed his arm. "You're skin and bones. I'll fatten you up!" she snorted, locking him in a cage.

"You can do the housework,"
she told Gretel grimly, "then
I'll make a meal of you too!"
As luck would have it, the witch
had very weak eyes.
"Let me feel your finger!" she
would say to Hansel every day, to
check if he were any fatter.
But Gretel had given him a
chicken bone and smeared the
witch's eyeglasses with butter.
When the old woman went to
touch his finger, he held out the
bone instead.
"Much too thin!" she would
complain.

One day the witch grew tired
of waiting. "Light the oven,"
she told Gretel. "We're going
to have a tasty boy for
dinner!" A little later the
impatient old crone snapped,
"Run and see if the oven is
hot yet!"
Gretel returned, whimpering,
"I can't tell if it's hot
enough, yet."
"Nitwit!" the witch screamed.
"I'll see for myself." She bent
down to peer inside the oven.
Gretel gave her a tremendous

push and slammed the door shut!
There was a screech and a sizzle, and that was the end of the witch.
Gretel ran to free her brother. Just to be on the safe side, they fastened the oven door with a large padlock.
The children feasted on the candy house until they discovered a huge chocolate egg. They broke off a piece. There inside lay a treasure chest of gold coins!
"We'll take the coins with us," said Hansel. The two children filled a large basket with food and set off through the forest in search of their home. Luck was with them, and on the second day they saw their father coming toward them, weeping.
"Thank God I have found you!" he cried. "Your stepmother is dead. Come home with me now, my dear children!"
Hansel and Gretel hugged their father with all their might.
"Promise you'll never desert us again," said Gretel.
"Look, Father," said Hansel, opening the chest. "We're rich now. You'll never have to chop wood again!"
And so they all lived happily together ever after.

The Seven Crows

Once upon a time . . . far away amid high mountains, there was a green valley with a clear stream running through it. Here a woodsman had built his house. He lived there with his wife, seven sons, and one daughter.

The woodsman was often away, and his wife had a hard time bringing up the children alone. The daughter was kind, pretty, and helpful. But the boys were rude, disobedient, and quarrelsome. They had no respect for their mother, and she was at her wits' end.

The poor woman kept her sorrow to herself instead of telling her husband, not realizing that it only made things worse. The boys' sister suffered most. She loved her brothers, despite their detestable behavior, but most of all she loved her mother.

One day the seven boys did the wickedest thing yet. In the woods grew a dangerous grass that made animals' stomachs swell.

The woodsman had always warned his sons not to let the goats eat it. The cruel boys filled a bag with the grass and mixed it with the animals' fodder. Soon, the goats and even the cow fell ill. Their stomachs swelled and they couldn't stand up.

"What will we do for milk? We won't be able to make any cheese!" cried the mother. "How will we survive?"

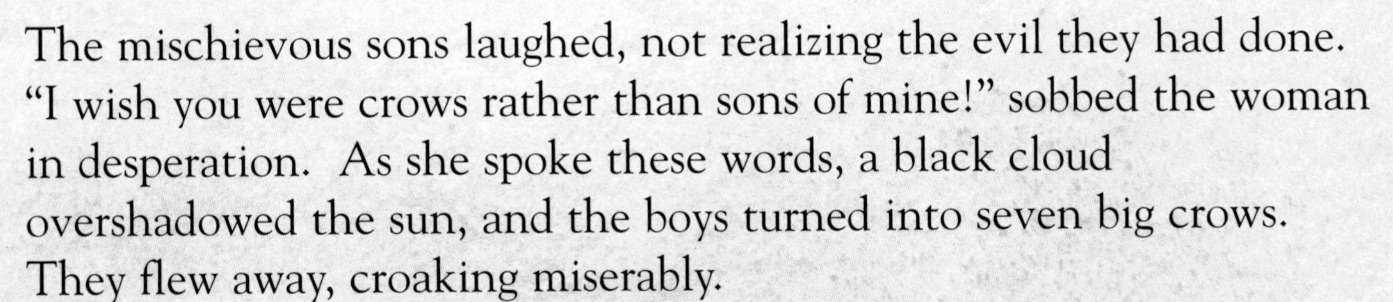

The mischievous sons laughed, not realizing the evil they had done. "I wish you were crows rather than sons of mine!" sobbed the woman in desperation. As she spoke these words, a black cloud overshadowed the sun, and the boys turned into seven big crows. They flew away, croaking miserably.

The woman was filled with fear and remorse. When the father came back from work the next day, he was shocked and saddened by the news of his sons' behavior and their terrible fate. He tried to comfort his wife, telling her it wasn't her fault. All the same, the house was filled with gloom.

A long time passed and the little girl grew older. She still remembered her brothers and rarely smiled. One day she asked her mother's permission to go and look for them. "I'll find them. Please let me go!" The mother couldn't resist her daughter's pleas, and the little girl left home with a small bundle of provisions.

For two days she walked through the woods, climbing toward the mountains. Soon she had no more food. Her clothes were torn and she was cold and tired. At dawn on the third day, she came upon a strange cottage in the mist. Something drew her to the house, despite its uninviting appearance. Inside, she found a low table with seven bowls on it, and her heart beat very fast.

Maybe she had found what she was looking for! There was a large pot full of oatmeal on the fire. The little girl was very hungry, so she poured some into a bowl and gulped it down.
Then she went upstairs. There she found seven tiny beds. Tears rose to her eyes as she realized her search was at an end. Exhausted by the journey, she lay down on one of the beds and fell asleep.
Some time later, seven chattering crows pushed open the front door and sat down at the table.
"Someone's been eating our oatmeal," said one of the crows, inspecting the dirty bowl.
"But who would ever come up here?" said another.

When the crows had finished eating they pulled on their sleeping caps and went upstairs. How surprised they were to find a little girl in one of the beds! One of the crows pecked delicately at a braid. "But this is . . . our sister!" they cried. At that moment, the little girl

opened her eyes. The sight of the crows scared her at first. But then she jumped up and held out her arms.
"I've found you! I've found you!" she cried joyfully.
"Will you come home with me?" she asked.
"We'd love to go back," replied the seven crows sadly, "and we're sorry for our evil ways. But how can we show ourselves to our parents like this?"
"Mother keeps crying and thinking of you," the little girl insisted, and soon she had convinced her brothers to make the journey.
"There's no need to walk over the mountains," said the brothers.
"We'll fly there and carry you."
As they were about to leave, the youngest brother called,
"Wait a minute! Let's bring Mother all the sparkling stones we've found." "They might be precious, you know," added another brother.
"When we crows see a sparkle, we can't help snapping it up."

"How beautiful!" said the little girl when the crows showed her their bag of treasure. She tucked it carefully in her pocket.
The crows took hold of her tightly, and they all rose up in the air. What a different place the world looked from above! At first the little girl felt very nervous, but her brothers held her firmly. By and by they flew over the valley, the stream, and the little house where they were born. The farmyard was deserted when they landed.
"You wait here and I'll go and call Mother," said the little girl.
She slipped silently into the kitchen.
Her mother sat at the table weeping.
"I'm back and I have a big surprise!" cried the little girl, hugging her mother.

The poor woman was so happy that she didn't know whether to laugh or cry. When she saw the crows in the farmyard she recognized them at once.

"My poor sons! I missed you so much. Why did I utter that curse?"

"We regret our wickedness too," clamored the crows. Suddenly their voices changed, and instead of seven crows, there stood seven boys.

The father, who had heard voices, came running from the house.

"My children!" he cried, embracing his seven lost sons and his dear daughter.

The sparkling stones turned out to be precious after all, and from that day forward, the family prospered.

The Golden Fish

Once upon a time . . . there was a poor fisherman who lived in a humble cottage near the sea. One day, he set off as usual with his load of nets to go fishing.

"Don't dare come home empty-handed!" shouted his nagging wife.

Down on the shore, he stood on a rock and threw his net into the sea. Something shiny caught his eye.

"What a strange fish!" he muttered, picking up a golden shape from the net. His amazement grew when he heard the fish speak.

"Kind fisherman, let me go! I am the son of the Sea King, and if you free me I will grant any wish you care to make!"

Alarmed, the fisherman tossed the fish back into the water.

But when he reached home his wife scolded him soundly.

"You should have asked for something. Go back to the beach and wish for a new washtub. Just look at the state of our old thing!"
The poor man went back to the rock. As soon as he called the fish, it popped its head out of the water.
"Were you calling me?"
The fisherman explained what his wife wanted.
"You were good to me," replied the fish. "Go home and you'll find your wish has come true."
Certain that his wife would be pleased, the fisherman hurried home. But the minute he opened the door, his wife screeched, "So it really is a magic fish! You can't possibly be content with a washtub . . .

. . . go straight back and wish for a new house!"
The fisherman hurried back to the shore. "I wonder if the fish will come again?" he muttered. "Little fish! Little fish!" he called from the water's edge.

"Here I am! What do you want this time?" he heard it ask.
"Well, my wife would like —"
"I can imagine!" remarked the fish. "What does she want now?"
"A big house," stammered the fisherman.
"All right! Since you were kind to me, you shall have your wish!"
The fisherman lingered on the way home, enjoying the feeling of making his wife happy. But as he caught sight of the roof of the splendid new house, his wife rushed up to him in a fury.

"Look here! Now that we know how powerful this fish is, we can't be content with a mere house. Run back and ask for a real palace! And fine clothes! Jewels, too!" This request upset the fisherman greatly. However, he had been henpecked for so many years that he couldn't say no to his wife.
He trudged back to the water's edge.

Full of doubt, he stood on the rock and called the little fish, but the sea began to get very rough.
Quite some time passed before the fish leapt from the waves. "I'm sorry to trouble you again," said the fisherman, much embarrassed.

"My wife has had second thoughts. She'd like a palace, and fine clothes and jewels as well."

Again the fish granted the fisherman's wishes, but it seemed less friendly than before. The fisherman turned homeward, relieved to have his wife's demands satisfied.

What a magnificent palace home was! At the top of a flight of steps stood his wife, dressed like a great lady, dripping in jewels.

"Go back and ask for —" she began impatiently. But the fisherman interrupted her.

"What? With such a fine palace! We must be content with what we have. Don't you think you're asking too much?"

“Do as you’re told,” snapped the wife. “Ask the fish to make me an Empress!” The poor fisherman set off unhappily for the seashore. A storm had blown up, and terrible flashes of lightning lit up the black sky. Kneeling on the rock amid the spray, the fisherman called to the little fish.

When it came, he told of his wife’s latest demand. But this time, after listening in silence, the golden fish disappeared beneath the waves without saying a word.

A great flash of lightning shot through the sky, and the fisherman saw that the palace had vanished without a trace. The humble cottage stood where it had always been.

His wife was waiting for him in tears.

“It serves you right!” grumbled the fisherman. Deep in his heart, however, he was glad that everything had returned to normal.

Each day after that he went fishing, but never again did he see the golden fish.

THE MUSICIANS OF BREMEN

Once upon a time . . . an old donkey was ill-treated by his master. He decided to run away, and when he heard that Bremen was looking for singers with the town band, he thought that someone with a fine braying voice like his might be accepted.
As he went along the road, the donkey met a skinny dog.
"Come with me. If you have a good bark, you'll find a job with the band too. Just wait and see!"
A little later, an old cat no longer able to catch mice joined them and the three of them set off towards town. As they passed a farmyard, they met a rooster who was crowing to the skies.
"You sing well," they told him. "What are you so happy about?"
"Happy?" muttered the rooster with tears in his eyes.

"They want to put me in the pot and make soup of me. I'm singing as hard as I can, for tomorrow I'll be gone." But the donkey told him, "Come with us. With your voice, you'll be famous in Bremen!" Now there were four of them. The way was long, night fell, and they found themselves in a thick forest.

Suddenly, in the distance they saw a light. It came from a little cottage and they crept up to the window ledge. The dog jumped on the donkey's back, the cat climbed onto the dog and the rooster flew on top of the cat to watch what was going on inside.

Now, the cottage was the hideaway of a gang of bandits who were celebrating their latest robbery. The hungry donkey and his friends

became excited when they saw the food on the table. The donkey stuck his head through the window and toppled his three friends onto the lamp. The light went out and the room rang with the braying of the donkey, who had cut his nose on the glass, the barking of the dog, the snarling of the cat, and the screeching of the rooster.

The bandits fled screaming, “The devil! The devil!” The four friends gobbled up the food. Later, one of the bandits crept back to the house. He opened the door, and stepped towards the fire. Mistaking the glow of the cat’s eyes for burning coals, he thrust a candle between them and the cat sank its claws into the bandit’s face. The man fell backwards onto the dog, dropping his gun, which went off, and the animal’s sharp teeth sank into his leg. The donkey gave a kick, sending the man flying through the doorway.

“Run!” screamed the bandit. “A horrible witch scratched my face, a devil bit me on the leg and a monster beat me with a stick!” But the other bandits had fled.

And so the donkey, the dog, the cat and the rooster took over the house. With the money left behind by the bandits, they always had food on the table, and lived happily for many years.

Fairy Tales of
Hans Christian Andersen

Once upon a time . . . there was a very good writer living in Denmark named Hans Christian Andersen. He wrote his first collection of fairy tales, entitled *Tales, Told for Children*, in 1835, and continued to write popular and interesting fairy tales in a new and innovative style until the 1870s. Andersen was very careful to include dialogue in his stories as it was spoken by the people of his time, and this made his stories especially attractive to readers in Denmark, and around the world.

Hans Christian Andersen, above right, was born in Denmark in 1805. Below, a view of the port of Copenhagen circa 1800. At left, a footsoldier of the Danish army walks by, with other people of the time.

Good and Evil - Andersen created very detailed portraits of the good and evil characters in his stories. He also felt strongly for unlucky and unhappy characters, and these figure often in his tales. Although some of his stories are very sad (such as "The Little Matchgirl") others are happy and show an underlying faith that good will prevail. Will the Tin Soldier live happily ever after with the ballerina? Will the Ugly Duckling find his friends?

Above, a typical study in the mid-1800s. An oil lamp was used for light, and documents were written by hand, like the manuscript above. Below, two of Andersen's most well-known characters: The Tin Soldier and The Little Mermaid.

A Very Talented Fellow . . . Andersen studied at the University of Copenhagen. He was a successful writer of fiction for adults, and he wrote for the theatre as well. He also wrote many autobiographical novels, which were well received.

The Ugly Duckling

Once upon a time . . . down on a farm, lived a duck family. Mother Duck had been sitting on some new eggs. One nice morning, the eggs hatched and out popped six ducklings.

But one egg was bigger than the rest, and it didn't hatch. Mother Duck couldn't recall laying that seventh egg. How did it get there? But before she had time to think about it, the last egg finally hatched. A strange looking duckling with gray feathers, that should have been yellow, gazed at Mother Duck.

"I can't understand how this ugly duckling can be one of mine!" she said to herself, shaking her head. The gray duckling wasn't pretty, and since he ate far more than his brothers, he was outgrowing them.

As the days went by, the poor ugly duckling became more and more unhappy.

His brothers didn't want to play with him, he was so clumsy, and all the farmyard folks laughed at him. He felt sad and lonely.

"Poor little ugly duckling!" Mother Duck would say.

"Why are you so different from the others?" The ugly duckling felt worse and worse.

"Nobody loves me!"

Then one day, at sunrise, he ran away from the farmyard.
He stopped at a pond and began to question all the other birds.
"Do you know of any ducklings with gray feathers like mine?"

But everyone shook their heads.
"We don't know anyone as ugly as you." He went to another pond, where a pair of large geese gave him the same answer to his question.

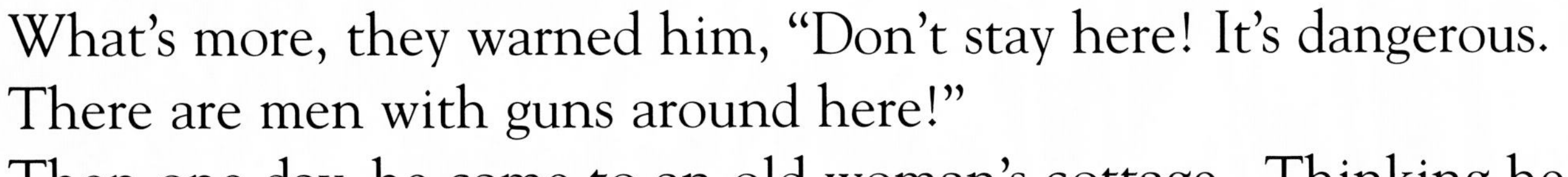

What's more, they warned him, "Don't stay here! It's dangerous. There are men with guns around here!"
Then one day, he came to an old woman's cottage. Thinking he was a goose, she caught him and put him in a cage.

"I hope it lays plenty of eggs!" said the old woman. But the ugly duckling laid not a single egg. The hen kept frightening him, "If you don't lay eggs, the old woman will wring your neck and pop you in the pot!" And the cat chimed in, "Hee! Hee! I hope the woman cooks you soon, then I can gnaw at your bones!"
The poor ugly duckling was so scared that he lost his appetite, though the old woman kept stuffing him with food and grumbling, "If you won't lay eggs,

at least hurry up and get plump!" "Oh, dear me!" moaned the terrified duckling. "I'll die of fright first!"
Then one night, finding the cage door ajar, he escaped.
At dawn, he found himself in a thick bed of reeds. There was plenty of food, and the duckling began to feel a little happier, though he was lonely. One day at sunrise, he saw a flight of beautiful birds wing overhead. White, with long slender necks, yellow beaks and large wings, they were migrating south.
"If only I could look like they do!" said the duckling.
Winter came and the water in the reed bed froze. The poor duckling was left to seek food in the snow. He dropped exhausted to the ground, but a farmer found him. "I'll take him home to my children. They'll look after him."
The duckling was showered with kindly care at the farmer's house. By springtime, he had grown so

big that the farmer decided,
"I'll set him free by the pond!"
That was when the duckling saw
his reflection in the water.
"Goodness! How I've changed!
I hardly recognize myself!"
The flight of swans winged north
again and glided onto the pond.
When the duckling saw them,
he realized he was one of their
kind, and soon made friends.
One day, as he swam majestically
with his fellow swans, he heard
children on the river bank exclaim,
"Look at that young swan!
He's the finest of them all!" And he almost burst with happiness.

The Story of Thumbelina

Once upon a time . . . there lived a woman who had no children. She dreamed of having a little girl, but time went by, and her dream never came true.

She decided to visit a witch, who gave her a magic grain of barley. She planted it in a flower pot. The very next day, the grain had turned into a lovely tulip. The woman softly kissed its petals, and as though by magic, the flower opened. Inside sat a tiny girl, no bigger than a thumb. The woman called her Thumbelina.

She had a walnut shell for a bed, violet petals for her mattress and a rose petal blanket. One night, as she lay fast asleep in her walnut shell, a large toad hopped in through the window.

As the toad gazed down at Thumbelina, she said to herself, “How pretty she is! She’d make the perfect bride for my son!”
She picked up Thumbelina, walnut shell and all, and hopped back to the pond. Her fat, ugly son was very pleased. But mother toad was afraid that her pretty prisoner might run away. So she carried Thumbelina out to a lily pad in the middle of the pond, and left her there.
Thumbelina was all alone. She felt so sad.
She knew she would never be able to escape the two horrid toads. All she could do was cry and cry.
A passing butterfly overheard the little girl’s sobs, and decided to rescue her. “Throw me the end of your belt! I’ll help you get away!”

Thumbelina was free at last. But other dangers lay ahead. A large beetle snatched Thumbelina and took her to his home at the top of a leafy tree. "Isn't she pretty?" he said to his friends. But they pointed out that she was far too different.

So the beetle took her back down the tree and set her free. All summer long Thumbelina wandered among the flowers and through the long grass. But soon winter set in and she felt terribly cold and hungry. One day, as Thumbelina roamed through the bare meadows, she met a large spider who promised to help her. He took her to a hollow tree where his family lived and brought her some dried chestnuts to eat. But just as before, Thumbelina had to leave the spiders' house because she was not like them.

As she wandered, shivering with the cold, she came across a little

cottage made of twigs and dead leaves. She knocked, and a field mouse opened the door. "What are you doing outside in such weather?" he asked. "Come in and warm yourself." The field mouse's house was cozy and stocked with food. Thumbelina finally had a home. One day the field mouse said a friend was coming to visit them. "He's a very rich mole, and has a lovely house. He needs company and he'd like to marry you!" But Thumbelina did not like the idea; she did not like it at all.

When the mole came, he fell in love with the beautiful little girl, and invited Thumbelina and the field mouse to visit him. To their surprise, they came upon a swallow in the mole's tunnel. It looked dead. The mole nudged it with his foot, saying, "That'll teach her! She should have come underground instead of darting about the sky all summer!" Later, Thumbelina crept back unseen to the tunnel. Every day the little girl nursed the swallow and gave it food.

"It's very kind of you to take care of me," the swallow said. In the spring, the swallow was able to fly away.

All summer Thumbelina did her best to avoid marrying the mole . . . she would have to live underground forever! On the eve of her wedding, she asked to spend a day in the open air. As she gently stroked a flower, she heard a familiar song from overhead. "Come with me!" cried the swallow. Thumbelina held on to her feathered friend, and the bird soared into the sky.

They flew until they reached a country of flowers. There she met a tiny, white-winged fairy; he was the King of the Flower Fairies. Instantly, he asked her to marry him. Thumbelina said "Yes!" and sprouting tiny white wings, she became the Flower Queen!

The Tin Soldier

Once upon a time . . . there was a little boy who had a lot of toys. One of his favorite games was the battle with the tin soldiers. One of the soldiers, however, had just one leg. The boy always placed this little soldier in the front lines, encouraging him to be the bravest of all the tin soldiers. The child did not know that, at night, the toys became animated and talked amongst themselves.
It often happened that, when lining up the soldiers after playing with them, the little boy would forget about the little tin soldier and would leave him with all the other toys. That is how the little tin soldier made the acquaintance of the pretty tin ballerina. The two of them became great friends, and pretty soon the little soldier fell in love with the ballerina. But he could never find the

courage to declare his love to her. When the child placed him in the front lines, the little soldier hoped that the ballerina would notice how brave he was. And when the ballerina asked the soldier if he had been afraid, he proudly answered, "No!"

One night, the jack-in-the-box said to him, "Hey! Don't look at the ballerina like that!" But the ballerina said, "Don't listen to him; he is jealous. I am very happy to talk to you."

The little tin figurines were both too shy to speak of their love.

One day they got separated. The boy picked up the tin soldier and placed him on the window sill.

"You stay here and watch for the enemy," he said.

Then the boy played inside with the other soldiers.

Suddenly a storm came up and knocked the little soldier head first off the window sill. It rained hard and soon there were big puddles everywhere. The storm stopped as suddenly as it had begun and two boys came out to play. They were hopping over the puddles when one noticed the little tin soldier stuck in the mud. He picked him up and put him in his pocket. On the other side of the street, the gutter was overflowing and the current carried a little paper boat.
"Let's put the little soldier in the boat and make him a sailor," said the boy. The whirling gutter flowed into a sewer and the little boat was carried down the drain.

The water was deep and muddy. Rats gnashed their teeth as the boat flowed by. It was about to sink, but the little soldier was not afraid. The little tin soldier realized his end was near. "I will never see my sweet little ballerina again!" he said to himself. Suddenly, a huge mouth swallowed the little tin soldier.

He found himself in the stomach of a large fish.
The fish did not have time to digest his meal, because soon after he was caught in the net of a fisherman and was taken to the market. Meanwhile, a cook (who worked in the same house where the little soldier used to live) was at the market. "This fish will be perfect for tonight's guests," she said.
When the cook slit the belly of the fish to clean it, she found the little tin soldier. She ran to find the boy.
"That's my soldier!" the little boy cheered. "I wonder how he got into the fish's belly?"
The little boy placed the soldier on the mantle, right next to the ballerina. The little soldier and the ballerina were very happy to be

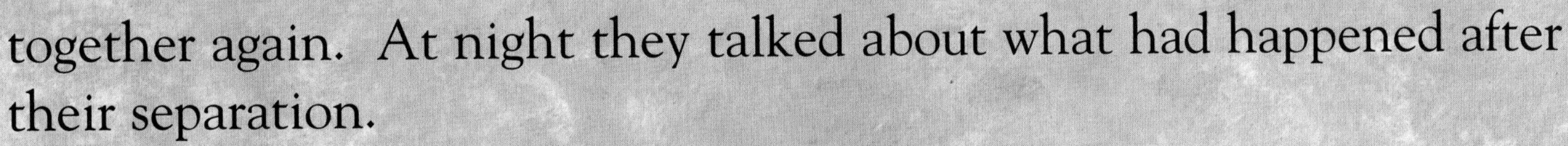

together again. At night they talked about what had happened after their separation.

But fate had another surprise in store for them.

One day, a sudden gust of wind knocked the ballerina over and she fell into the fireplace. When the little soldier saw her fall, he was frightened. Fire is the greatest enemy of tin figurines.

Rocking back and forth on his one leg, the little soldier tried to move. He kept trying until he fell into the fire as well.

The two figurines were reunited in their misfortune. They were so close to each other now, that their metal bases melted together, into the shape of a heart.

Just then, the little boy saw the two little figurines in the fire, and he quickly kicked them out of the flames with his foot. From then on, the soldier and the ballerina were happily joined together on their shared base, shaped like a heart.

THE EMPEROR'S NEW CLOTHES

Once upon a time . . . there lived a vain emperor whose only worry in life was to dress in elegant clothes. He changed clothes almost every hour, and loved to show them off to his people. Word of the emperor's grandeur spread through his kingdom and beyond. Hearing of the emperor's vanity, two scoundrels decided to take advantage of it.

They presented themselves at the palace gates.

"We are wonderful tailors who have invented a way of weaving cloth so light and fine that it can't be seen by anyone who is too stupid to appreciate it," they told the guard.

The guard sent for the court chamberlain, the chamberlain notified the prime minister, and the prime minister ran to the emperor with the incredible news. The emperor, consumed by curiosity, decided to see the two scoundrels.

"Your Majesty, besides being invisible, this cloth will be woven in colors and patterns especially for you," said the wily tailors.

The emperor gave the two men

a bag of gold in exchange for their promise to begin work immediately.
The tailors asked for a loom and a quantity of silk and gold thread, and pretended to set to work. The emperor thought his money well spent.
Not only would he get a new suit, he would find out which of his subjects were stupid!
A few days later, he called in

the prime minister, a man known for his common sense, and said, "Go and see how the work is getting on."
"We're almost finished," said the two scoundrels, welcoming the prime minister. "Just look at these colors, and feel the softness of the material!"
The old man bent over the loom. "I can't see a thing," he said to himself. "That must mean I'm stupid!"
He coughed nervously.

"Ahem! What a marvelous fabric! I shall certainly tell the emperor."

The two scoundrels rubbed their hands gleefully, and requested more golden thread. Before long, they arrived at the royal apartments, ready to take measurements for the suit.

"Come in, come in," said the emperor eagerly.

The scoundrels bowed low and pretended to stagger under the weight of the cloth. "Here it is, Your Majesty. What do you think of it? Just look at the rich colors and feel how soft it is!"

Of course the emperor could see and feel nothing. "I must be stupid!" he thought in a panic. "I'd better pretend to see it so that no one will know." And so he praised the beautiful cloth, unaware that everyone around him was thinking the very same thing about themselves!

The two scoundrels took the emperor's measurements. They set to work, busily cutting the air with scissors and stitching together pieces of nothing at all.

After a while, they said, "Your Majesty, you'll have to take off your clothes to try on your new suit." They draped the invisible garments about him and held up a mirror.

The emperor was dreadfully embarrassed, but as the bystanders seemed to notice nothing amiss, he felt relieved. "Yes — ahhh hmmm — a beautiful suit," he declared.

"Your Majesty," said the prime minister, "the people are anxious to see this amazing fabric and to admire your new suit."
The emperor was doubtful about showing himself naked to his subjects. "Oh well," he comforted himself, "only the stupid ones will know."
"All right," he said grandly. "I will grant the people's wish."
He summoned his open carriage and a stately procession was formed. In front walked the court officials, anxiously scrutinizing the faces in the street.
All the people had gathered in the main square to get a better look, and to find out how stupid their neighbors might be.
As the emperor passed, a murmur of admiration arose from the crowd, "Look at the emperor's new clothes. How fine they are!"

They all tried to conceal their disappointment and dismay at not seeing the clothes.

By and by, however, a child ran up to the carriage. "Why, the emperor is naked!" he blurted out.

"Fool!" his father scolded, dragging the child away. But the boy's remark had been overheard, and was repeated again and again until everyone shouted, "The boy is right. The emperor is naked!"

The emperor realized to his shame that the people were right, but thought it better to continue the procession. And so he stood stiffly in his carriage all the way home, resolving never to be vain again.

As for the two scoundrels, they made off with all the gold and the precious thread, laughing all the way.

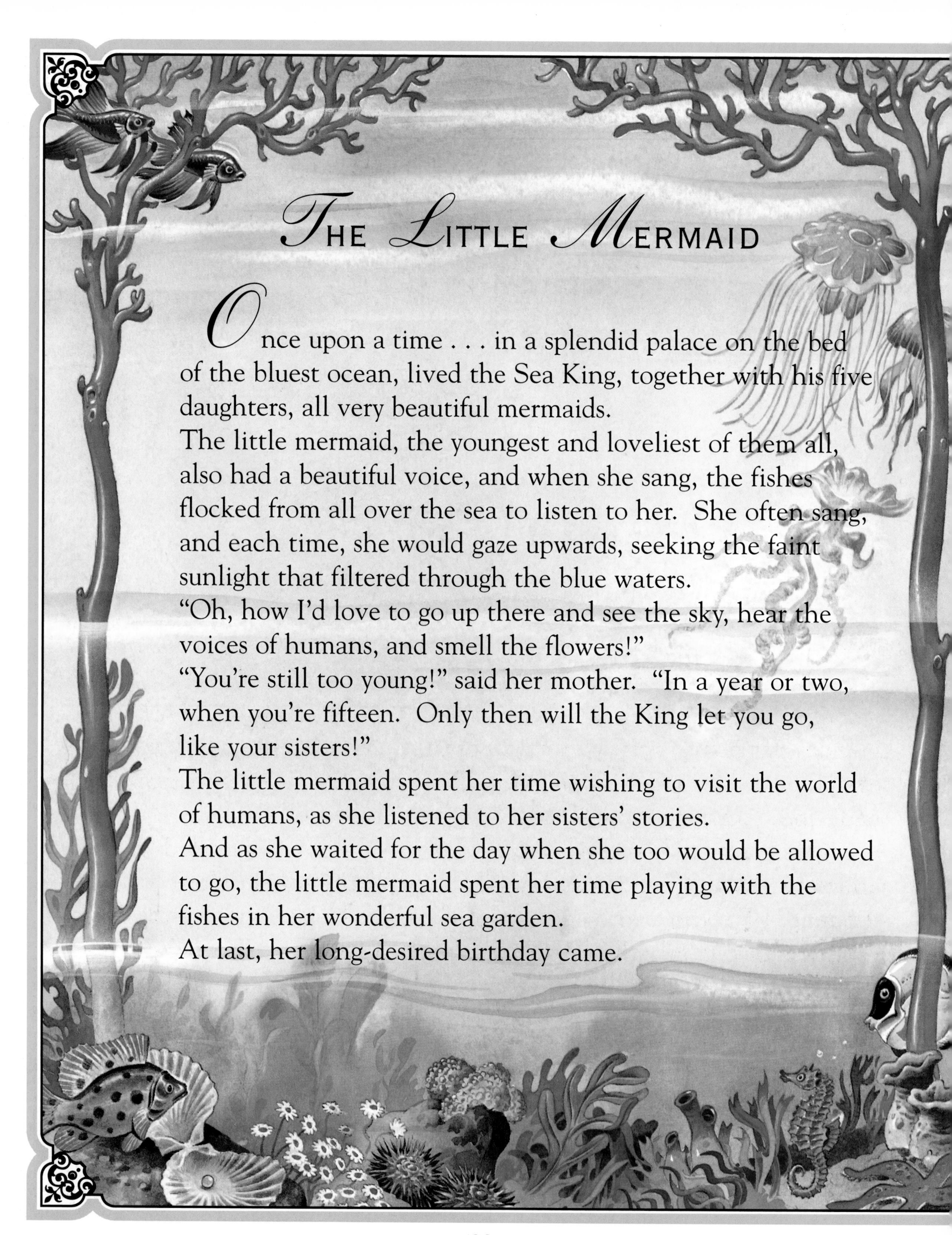

The Little Mermaid

Once upon a time . . . in a splendid palace on the bed of the bluest ocean, lived the Sea King, together with his five daughters, all very beautiful mermaids.

The little mermaid, the youngest and loveliest of them all, also had a beautiful voice, and when she sang, the fishes flocked from all over the sea to listen to her. She often sang, and each time, she would gaze upwards, seeking the faint sunlight that filtered through the blue waters.

"Oh, how I'd love to go up there and see the sky, hear the voices of humans, and smell the flowers!"

"You're still too young!" said her mother. "In a year or two, when you're fifteen. Only then will the King let you go, like your sisters!"

The little mermaid spent her time wishing to visit the world of humans, as she listened to her sisters' stories.

And as she waited for the day when she too would be allowed to go, the little mermaid spent her time playing with the fishes in her wonderful sea garden.

At last, her long-desired birthday came.

Her father called her and, stroking her long golden hair, slipped a lovely carved flower into her locks.
"There! Now you can go to the surface. You'll breathe air and see the sky. But remember! It's not our world! We're children of the sea and have no soul, as humans do. Be careful and keep away from them; they can only bring bad luck!"
The little mermaid kissed her father and darted smoothly towards the surface of the sea. Suddenly she popped out of the water. How wonderful! For the first time, she saw the great blue sky.
As dusk began to fall, the first stars were peeping out and twinkling. "It's so lovely!" she exclaimed happily. Then the little mermaid saw a ship slowly sailing towards the rock on which she was sitting.
The sailors dropped anchor and went about their work aboard, lighting the lanterns for the night.

"I'd love to speak to them!" she said to herself. But she gazed sadly at her long tail, and said to herself, "I can never be like them!" Aboard ship, a strange excitement was in the air, and a little later, the sky was filled with many-colored lights and the crackle of fireworks.

"Long live the captain! Hurrah for his twentieth birthday! Hurrah! Hurrah!" Then, the little mermaid caught sight of the young man in whose honor the celebration was being held. Tall and handsome, she could not take her eyes off him. The party went on, but the sea grew stormy. The black sky was torn by flashes of lightning, and the rising waves swept over the ship. Masts and sails toppled onto the deck, and the helpless ship sank.

The little mermaid had seen the young captain fall into the water, and she bravely swam to his rescue.

On the crest of a nearby wave, in an instant he was swept straight into her arms. The young man was unconscious and the mermaid held his head above water in the stormy sea. She clung to him for hours, trying to save his life.

Then, as suddenly as it had come up, the storm died away. At dawn, the little mermaid realized thankfully that land lay ahead.

She pushed the captain's body onto the shore, but unable to walk, she tried to warm the young captain with her own body. Then the sound of voices startled her and she slipped back into the water.

"Come quickly!" came a woman's voice. "There's a man here. Look, I think he's unconscious!"

"Let's take him up to the castle!" was the reply.

The first thing the young man saw when he opened his eyes again was the beautiful face of the youngest of a group of three ladies.

"Thank you for saving my life!" he murmured to the lovely unknown lady.

From the sea, the little mermaid watched the man turn towards the castle — he did not know that a mermaid had saved his life. Slowly swimming out to sea, the little mermaid felt that she had left behind something that she could never forget. As she swam down towards her father's palace, her sisters came to meet her. She started to tell her story, but a lump came to her throat and, bursting into tears, she fled to her room. She stayed there for days, refusing to see anyone. She knew that her love for the young captain was hopeless, for she was a mermaid and could never marry a human. Only the Witch of the Deeps could help her. The little mermaid decided to go and see her. "So, you want to get rid of your tail, do you? You'd like to have a pair of legs?"

said the nasty witch, from her cave.
"Be warned!" she went on. "You will suffer horribly. Every time you place your feet on the earth, you will feel dreadful pain!"
"It doesn't matter!" whispered the little mermaid. "As long as I can go back to him!"
"And that's not all!" exclaimed the witch. "In exchange for my spell, you must give me your lovely voice. You'll never be able to utter a word again! And if the man you love marries someone else, you will not be able to turn into a mermaid again. You will dissolve in water like foam on a wave!"
"All right!" said the little mermaid, eagerly taking a little jar holding the magic potion. The witch had told her that the young captain was actually a prince. The mermaid came out of the water not far from the castle. She pulled herself onto the beach, and drank the magic potion. An agonizing pain made her faint, and when she came to, she could see the face she loved, smiling down at her. The prince gently laid his cloak over her body.
"Don't be frightened!" he said. "You're quite safe! Where have you come from?"
But the little mermaid was now mute and could not reply.
"I'll take you to the castle and look after you," he said.
In the days that followed, the little mermaid started a new life. She wore splendid dresses and often went out on horseback with the prince. One evening, she was invited to a great ball.

However, as the witch had foretold, every step she took was torture. The little mermaid bravely put up with her suffering, so glad was she to be near her beloved prince. And though she could not speak to him, he was kind to her.
However, the young man's heart really belonged to the unknown lady he had seen as he lay on the shore, even though he had never seen her since then, for she had returned to her own land.
Even when he was in the company of the little mermaid, the unknown lady was in his thoughts. And the little mermaid, guessing that she was not his true love, suffered even more.
One day a huge ship sailed into the harbor. Together with the little mermaid, the prince went down to meet it.
And who stepped from the vessel, but the unknown lady. The prince rushed to greet her. The little mermaid felt herself turn to stone and a painful feeling pierced her heart: she was about to lose the prince forever. The unknown lady too had never forgotten the young man, and soon after, he asked her to marry him and she happily said, "Yes."
A few days after the wedding, the couple went for a voyage on the huge ship. The little mermaid too went on board, and the ship set sail. Night fell, and sick at heart over the loss of the prince, she went up on deck. She remembered the witch's words, and was now ready to give up her life and dissolve in the sea. Suddenly she heard a cry from the water and dimly saw her sisters in the darkness.
"Little mermaid! Here! It's us . . . your sisters! We've heard all about what happened! Look! Do you see this knife? It's magic! The witch gave it to us in exchange for our hair.

Take it! Kill the prince before dawn, and you will become a mermaid again!" She clasped the knife and entered the cabin where the prince and his bride lay fast asleep. She gazed at the young man's face, and then, she simply blew him a kiss before running back up on deck. When dawn broke, she threw the knife into the sea.

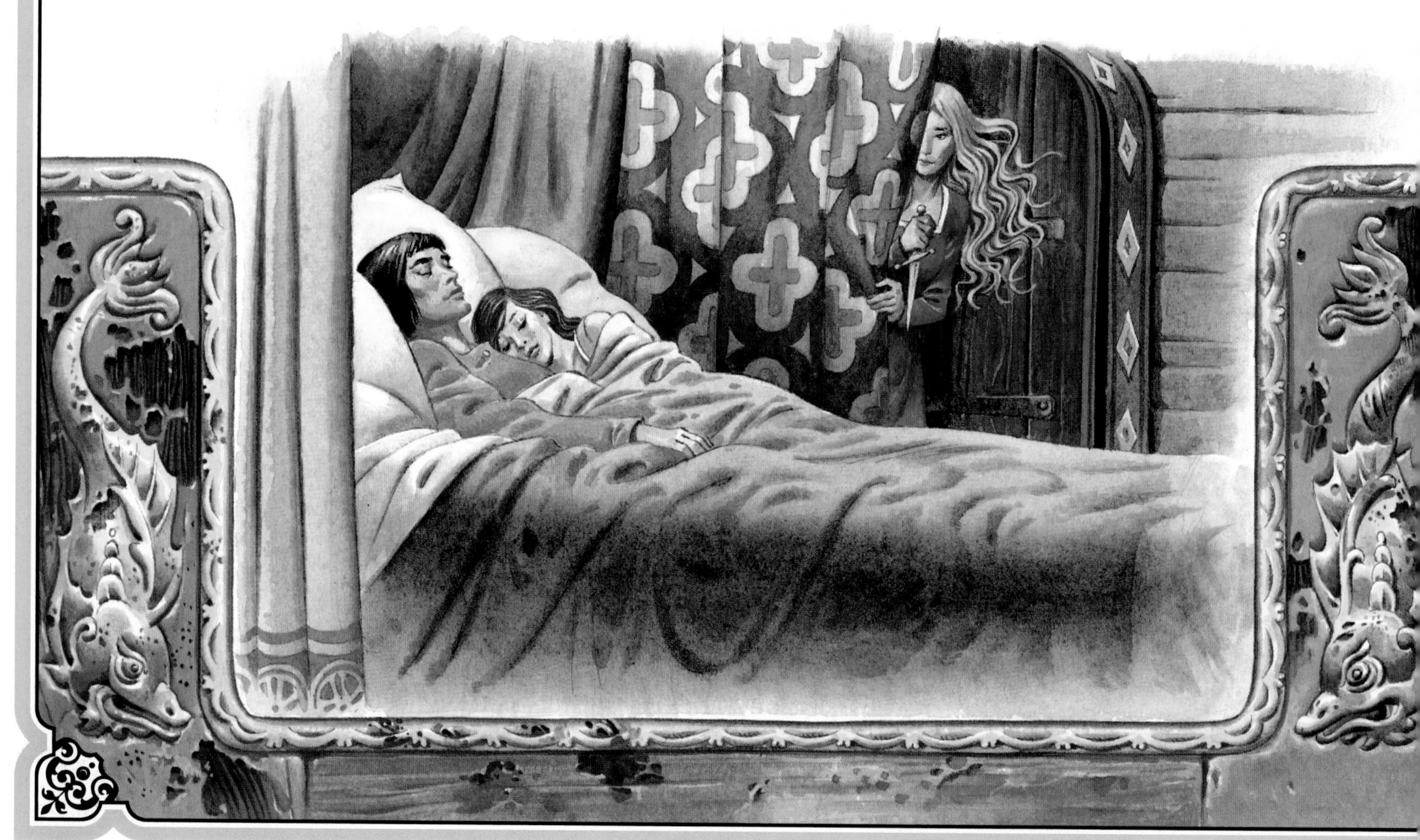

Then she dived into the waves, ready to turn into the foam of the sea and vanish.

As the sun rose over the horizon, the little mermaid turned towards it for the last time. Suddenly, as if by magic, a mysterious force drew her out of the water, and she felt herself lifted high into the sky. The clouds were tinged with pink, and the little mermaid heard a whisper through the tinkling of bells, "Little mermaid! Come with us . . ."

"Who are you?" asked the little mermaid, surprised to find she had recovered her voice. "Where am I?"

"You're with us in the sky. We're the fairies of the air! We take with us only those who have shown kindness to men!"

The little mermaid looked down towards the prince's ship, and felt tears come to her eyes.

The fairies of the air whispered to her, "Look! The earth flowers are waiting for our tears to turn into the morning dew! Come along with us!"

The Snow Queen

Once upon a time . . . an evil sorcerer made a magic mirror in which love was reflected as hate.

One day the mirror broke, and tiny pieces flew all over the world. If a sliver entered someone's eye or heart, that person became cold and hateful.

Karl and Gerda were two young children who loved each other dearly. Even the sweet pea that grew on Karl's windowsill spread across the street to entwine itself with Gerda's rose bush.

One winter day, as Karl sat on a window seat watching the snow drift down, he saw a large white flake land in the garden. Its lacy crystals grew and grew until a beautiful ice maiden stood where the flake had fallen.

Karl opened the window. As the cold air rushed in he was startled to hear the maiden speak his name. He closed the

window and sat down beside Gerda, who was reading a book.
"Something's pricking my eye!" he said.
Gerda looked, but saw nothing, for the splinter from the magic mirror had gone in deep.

From that day on, Karl became a hateful boy. Only Gerda still loved him, although he was rude and unkind in return.
One day, when Karl was playing in the snow, he heard bells jingling. He looked up and saw the beautiful maiden again, but this time she wore a coat with a large fur collar, and sat in a great, horse-drawn sleigh. Little did he know that this was the dreaded Snow Queen.
"Hitch your sled behind my sleigh, and I'll give you a wonderful ride," said the Snow Queen. Entranced, the little boy tied his sled to the sleigh. They sped away, and before long the great sleigh soared up in the air. Frightened, Karl clung to his sled until they landed on an immense white plain.
"Come and keep warm," said the Snow Queen invitingly.
Karl climbed into the sleigh. The Snow Queen kissed him, and as her icy lips touched his forehead, the little boy's heart froze and he forgot all about Gerda and his past life.
All winter Gerda looked for Karl, but he was nowhere to be found. When spring came, the rose and sweet pea trailed sadly, refusing to bloom or twine. At last, Gerda went down to the river.

“I will give you my red shoes if you tell me what happened to Karl,” Gerda told the river. She threw her shoes into the water but they floated back to the shore. Then Gerda climbed into a little boat and drifted away, hoping the river would take her to Karl.
At dusk, the boat came ashore in the midst of a wood.

Gerda climbed out and wandered away. Suddenly, a reindeer came through the trees and a crow flapped down on a branch.
"If you're looking for Karl, I saw him fly by on the Snow Queen's sleigh," said the crow.
"Where is he now?" cried Gerda.
The reindeer replied, "In Lapland. I will take you there."
Gerda climbed onto the reindeer's back, and it galloped northward until they came to the frozen tundra, lit by the fiery glow of the Northern Lights. As they neared the Snow Queen's castle, Gerda caught a glimpse of Karl. He was sitting on a rock staring coldly into space.

"Karl!" cried Gerda. But Karl stared straight ahead.
Gerda threw her arms around him and burst into tears.
Her teardrops fell on his eyes and ran down his chest. The warm tears melted Karl's heart, and he remembered Gerda and his past life. Then he too began to cry, and the hateful sliver of mirror floated out of his eye.
"Come!" cried Gerda. The reindeer carried the children home, and there they saw the rose and the sweet pea intertwine and blossom again, a sign of their everlasting friendship.

The Little Matchgirl

Once upon a time . . . a little girl tried to make a living by selling matches in the street. It was New Year's Eve and the snowy streets were deserted. From brightly lit windows came the sound of laughter and singing. People were getting ready to bring in the New Year. But the poor little matchseller, in her ragged dress and worn shawl, sat beside a fountain, shivering from the cold. She hadn't sold one box of matches all day. The little girl's fingers were frozen stiff. If only she could light a match! Her hands shaking, she took out a match and lit it. What a nice, warm flame! The little matchseller cupped her

hand over it, and as she did so, she magically saw in its light a brightly burning stove.

She held out her hands to the heat, but just then the match went out and the vision faded. The night seemed blacker than before and it was getting colder.

She struck another match on the wall, and this time, the glimmer turned the wall into a great sheet of crystal. Beyond that stood a fine table laden with food. The little matchgirl held out her arms toward the plates, but then the match went out and the magic faded. Poor thing! In just a few seconds she had caught a glimpse of everything that life had denied her: warmth and good things to eat.

Her eyes filled with tears.
She lit a third match and an even more wonderful thing happened: there stood a Christmas tree hung with hundreds of candles, glittering with tinsel and colored balls. “Oh, how lovely!” exclaimed the little matchgirl, holding up the match. Then, the match burned her finger and flickered out. The beautiful Christmas tree faded into the darkness.
Scarcely aware, the little matchgirl lit yet another match.

This time she saw her grandmother.
"Granny, stay with me!" she pleaded, as she lit one match after another, so that her grandmother would not disappear like all the other visions. Granny did not vanish, but gazed smilingly at her. Then she opened her arms and the little girl hugged her crying, "Granny, take me away with you!"
A cold day dawned and a pale sun shone on the fountain and the icy road. Close by lay the lifeless body of a little girl surrounded by burnt-out matches.
But the smile on her face was a sign that the little matchgirl was far away, in a place where there is neither cold, hunger, nor pain.

THE MAGIC TINDERBOX

Once upon a time . . . a brave soldier returned from the wars. In spite of his courage, his pockets were empty; his only possession was his sword. As he walked through a forest, he met a witch, who said to him, "I say, good soldier, would you like to earn a bag of money?" "Money? I'd do anything for money . . . ," the soldier replied.
"Good!" the witch went on. "It won't be difficult! All you have to do is go down that hollow tree till you reach a cave. There, you'll find three doorways. When you open the first door, you'll see a big dog with eyes like saucers, guarding a large chest of copper coins. Behind the second door lies a treasure of silver coins, guarded by a dog with eyes the size of millstones. When you open the third door, you'll come upon another dog, with eyes the size of a castle tower, beside a treasure of gold. Now, if you lay this old apron of mine before these dogs, they'll crouch on it and do you no harm. You'll be able to carry away all the coins you want." The soldier was suspicious, so he asked her,

"What do you want in return?"
"Just bring me back an old tinderbox my grandmother forgot long ago!" said the witch.
So the young soldier tied a rope round his waist and, not forgetting his trusty sword, he lowered himself into the hollow tree. To his surprise, he found the three doorways and the three dogs, just as the witch had said. Soon he was back, his pockets bulging with coins. Before he handed the tinderbox to the old witch, he asked,
"What do you want it for?" The witch hurled herself at him screaming, "Give it to me! Give it to me at once!"

The witch attacked him, and the soldier exclaimed, “So this is the thanks I get! Now I’ll show you!”

He undid the rope from around his waist and tied up the old woman. Then he went away. When he reached the town, he said to himself, “I can feast as much as I like — at last!” With his sudden wealth, the soldier felt like a prince. He bought a new pair of boots and he went to the best tailor in town. Lavish with his money, the soldier was surrounded by folk quick to tell him how to spend it — on a round of dances, fine carriages, and theaters. His money soon ran out and when this happened, his “friends” vanished. When the innkeeper discovered that the soldier could no longer pay his board, he put him out. So the soldier ended up in a garret and every day he had to tighten his belt a little more.

One evening, he realized he had never used the old witch's tinderbox. So he rubbed it, and as it sparked, the dog with eyes like saucers suddenly appeared. "Tell me your wish, sir," it said.
"B-bring me heaps of money!" stuttered the soldier in amazement.
A second later, the dog was back with a bag of coins.
When he rubbed the tinderbox twice, the dog with eyes like millstones stood before him, carrying silver coins. When he rubbed it three times, the third dog came carrying gold. Rich again, the soldier led the life of a fine gentleman.
While at the royal palace, the soldier discovered that the king would not allow anyone to meet his daughter, for he believed a prophecy that the princess' destiny was to marry a simple soldier.
That evening, the soldier rubbed the tinderbox.

“Bring me the princess!” he ordered. Immediately the dog returned with the princess, fast asleep. The soldier could not but kiss her.

The next morning, the girl told her parents that she had had a dream. Suspicious, the queen guarded her daughter, and the next evening, the dog was seen. The alarm sounded.

The king's guards arrested the soldier at dawn, and the king decided the soldier was to be hanged! When the day of execution came, a mob gathered around the scaffold. The soldier asked if he could smoke, and he rubbed the tinderbox three times. In a flash, the dogs appeared and leapt on the guards. Awestruck, the king bowed his head and whispered to the queen, "And so the prophecy comes true."

A short while later, the young soldier married the princess, and the tinderbox was rubbed, but this time to invite the three dogs to the splendid wedding.

Fairy Tales of ENGLAND

The History of the Fairy Tale - The first tales were told orally, passed from person to person; they were not written down in books. Characters and situations were often similar, and for this reason tales moved from country to country and from language to language. Animals were often present, and some element of the tale was always magical.

Jonathan Swift was born November 30, 1667 in Dublin, Ireland. He died in 1745.

In England in the 19th century . . . there was a new and important movement: the creation of literature specifically for children. Swift wrote slightly before this time, but Browning wrote during this very time period.

Above, Gulliver uses his size to assist him in his escape from Lilliput.

Left, in a time of much industry, young boys push carts of coal to the factory. In 1819, a law was passed in England prohibiting the hiring of children under nine years of age.

"The Pied Piper of Hamelin" - This work was published in 1842. It was originally written as a poem of over three hundred lines. However, the drama of the story was very evident and soon this tale of the piper, the children, and the town council's greed became a favorite of young readers everywhere.

Robert Browning was born on May 7, 1812 in London, England and died on December 12, 1889 in Venice, Italy. His wife was the poet Elizabeth Barrett Browning.

***Gulliver's Travels* -** This story of satire was published in 1726, and originally, it was not intended for children. In fact, it is a very long story, but the first two parts have become the most well-known in the world of children's literature. Swift's intention was to make fun of the social and political life in his country; he did so in such an imaginative way that he managed to create a children's classic at the same time.

Above, the Pied Piper, playing his magical pipe, drove away all of the rats from Hamelin.

Right, the velocipede became a fixture circa 1870. Newspapers also became very popular and among the most widely known was* The Times *of London.

Goldilocks and the Three Bears

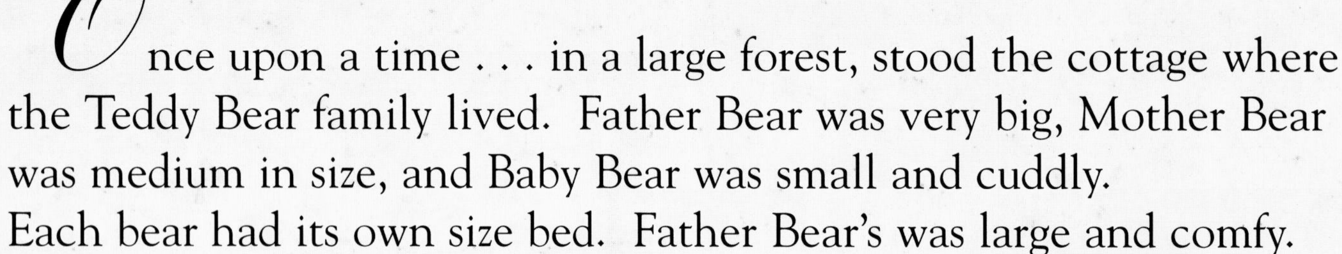

Once upon a time . . . in a large forest, stood the cottage where the Teddy Bear family lived. Father Bear was very big, Mother Bear was medium in size, and Baby Bear was small and cuddly.

Each bear had its own size bed. Father Bear's was large and comfy. Mother Bear's was medium in size, while Baby Bear had a fine little cherry wood bed.

Beside the fireplace stood a large carved chair for the head of the house, a blue velvet armchair for Mother Bear, and a very little chair for Baby Bear.

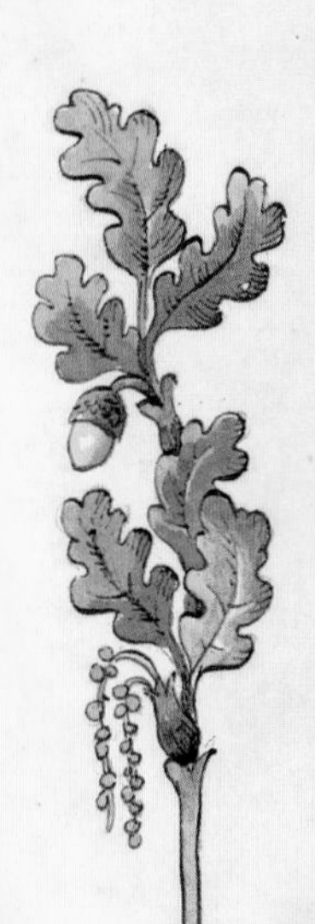

Neatly laid out on the kitchen table were three china bowls.
A large one for Father Bear, a smaller one for Mother Bear, and a little bowl for Baby Bear.
The neighbors were all very respectful to Father Bear and people raised their hats when he went by. Mother Bear had lots of friends. She visited them in the afternoons to exchange good advice and recipes for jam. Baby Bear, however, had hardly any friends.
This was partly because he was a bully and a pest and was always getting into mischief. Not far away lived a fair-haired little girl who had a similar nature to Baby Bear, only she was stuck-up as well, and though Baby Bear often asked her to come and play at his house, she always said no.
One day Mother Bear made a nice pudding. When it was ready, she said to the family, "It has to be left to cool now. That will take at least an hour. Why don't we go and visit the Beavers' new baby? Mother Beaver will be pleased to see us."
And so they set off along the path towards the river bank.

A short time later, the stuck-up little girl, whose name was Goldilocks, passed by the Bears' house as she picked flowers.
"Oh, what an ugly house the Bears have!" said Goldilocks to herself as she went down the hill.
"I'm going to peep inside! It won't be beautiful like my house, but I'm dying to see where Baby Bear lives."
The little girl tapped on the door.
Knock! Knock!
Not a sound . . .
"Anyone at home?" she called, peering around the door.
Then she went into the empty house and started to explore the kitchen.

"A pudding!" she cried.
"Quite nice! Quite nice!"
she murmured, spooning it
from Baby Bear's bowl.
In a twinkling, the bowl
lay empty on a messy table.
Goldilocks went on exploring.
"Now then, this must be
Father Bear's chair, this will be
Mother Bear's, and this one . . .
must belong to Baby Bear."
Goldilocks sat herself down
onto the little chair.
The leg broke and Goldilocks crashed to the floor!
Not in the least dismayed by the damage she had done,
she went upstairs.

There was no mistaking
which was Baby Bear's bed.
"Mm! Quite comfy!" she said.
"Not as nice as mine,
but nearly!"
Then she yawned. "I think
I'll lie down, only for a minute
. . . just to try the bed."

And in next to no time, Goldilocks lay fast asleep in Baby Bear's bed.
In the meantime, the Bears were on their way home.
From a distance, Father Bear noticed the door was ajar.
"Hurry!" he cried. "Someone is in our house . . . ."
Father Bear dashed into the kitchen. "I knew it! Somebody has gobbled up the pudding . . . ."

"And somebody has broken my chair!" wailed Baby Bear.
They all ran upstairs and tiptoed in amazement over to Baby Bear's bed. In it lay Goldilocks, sound asleep.
Baby Bear prodded her toe . . . . "Where am I?" shrieked the little girl, waking with a start. Taking fright at the scowling faces bending over her, she jumped out of bed and fled down the stairs.
As she ran away from the house, Baby Bear called from the door, "Don't run away! Come back! Come and play with me!"
From that day on, Goldilocks became a pleasant little girl. She made friends with Baby Bear and often went to his house. She invited him to her house too, and they remained good friends always.

JACK AND THE BEANSTALK

Once upon a time . . . there was a poor widow who lived with her son Jack in a little house. Their wealth consisted solely of a milking cow. When the cow had grown too old, the mother sent Jack to sell it. On his way to the market, the boy met a stranger. "I will give you five magic beans for your cow," the stranger offered. Jack thought this was such a good deal that he decided to accept. When he returned home, his mother was furious.
"What have you done? We needed the money to buy a calf. Now we don't have anything and we are even poorer . . .

. . . only a fool would exchange a cow for five beans!" she fumed.
Then she took the five beans and threw them out the window.
The next morning, when Jack stepped outside, he saw an amazing sight. A gigantic beanstalk, reaching far into the clouds, had grown overnight.
"The beans must have really been magic," Jack thought happily. Being curious, the boy climbed the plant, and reaching the top of the stalk, he found himself above the clouds. As he looked around at what he saw in amazement, Jack spotted a huge stone castle.

"I wonder who lives there," he thought. He cautiously stepped on the clouds and, when he saw that they held him up, he walked towards the castle. He knocked several times on the gigantic door.

"What are you doing here?" a thundering voice asked. The biggest woman he had ever seen was scowling at him. Jack could only say, "I am lost and I am very hungry." The woman, who liked children, looked at him kindly.

"Come in, quick. I will give you a bowl of milk. But be careful because my husband, the ogre, eats children. If you hear him coming, hide at once."

Jack was shaking with fear but, nonetheless, he went inside. He had almost finished drinking the milk when they heard a very loud noise.

"Fee fi fo fum! I smell the blood of an Englishman!" the ogre shouted.
"Quick, hide!" the woman whispered. "Do I smell a child in this room?" the ogre asked, sniffing and looking around.
"A child?" the woman repeated.

"You see and hear children everywhere. That's all you ever think about. Sit down and eat." The ogre filled a jug with wine and drank it with his dinner.

After his meal, the ogre counted his gold pieces and then fell asleep. Jack sneaked out, saw the gold pieces on the table, and filled a little bag full of them.

"I hope he won't see me, otherwise he'll eat me whole," Jack thought, shivering with fear.

With all the gold coins, he and his mother would be rich. Jack ran down the path over the clouds.

He arrived at the top of the giant beanstalk and began to descend as quickly as possible. When he finally reached the ground, he found his mother waiting for him.
"Where have you been, my son? Do you want me to die worrying? What kind of plant is this? What — "
Jack interrupted her, emptying the bag of gold pieces before her.
"You see, I did the right thing, exchanging that cow for the magic beans." Jack told his mother everything that had happened to him.
The gold pieces were spent to buy a lot of things Jack and his mother never had before. Mother and son were very happy. But before long, all the money was spent.
Jack decided to go back to the castle above the clouds. He went into the kitchen and hid once again. Shortly after, the ogre came in and sat down to eat.
After dinner, the ogre placed a hen on the table. The hen laid golden eggs! Jack waited for the ogre to fall asleep, then he jumped out, grabbed the hen and ran from the castle. The hen's squawking, however, woke up the ogre.
"Thief! Thief!" he shouted. But Jack was already far away.
Once again, he found his mother waiting for him at the foot of the beanstalk.

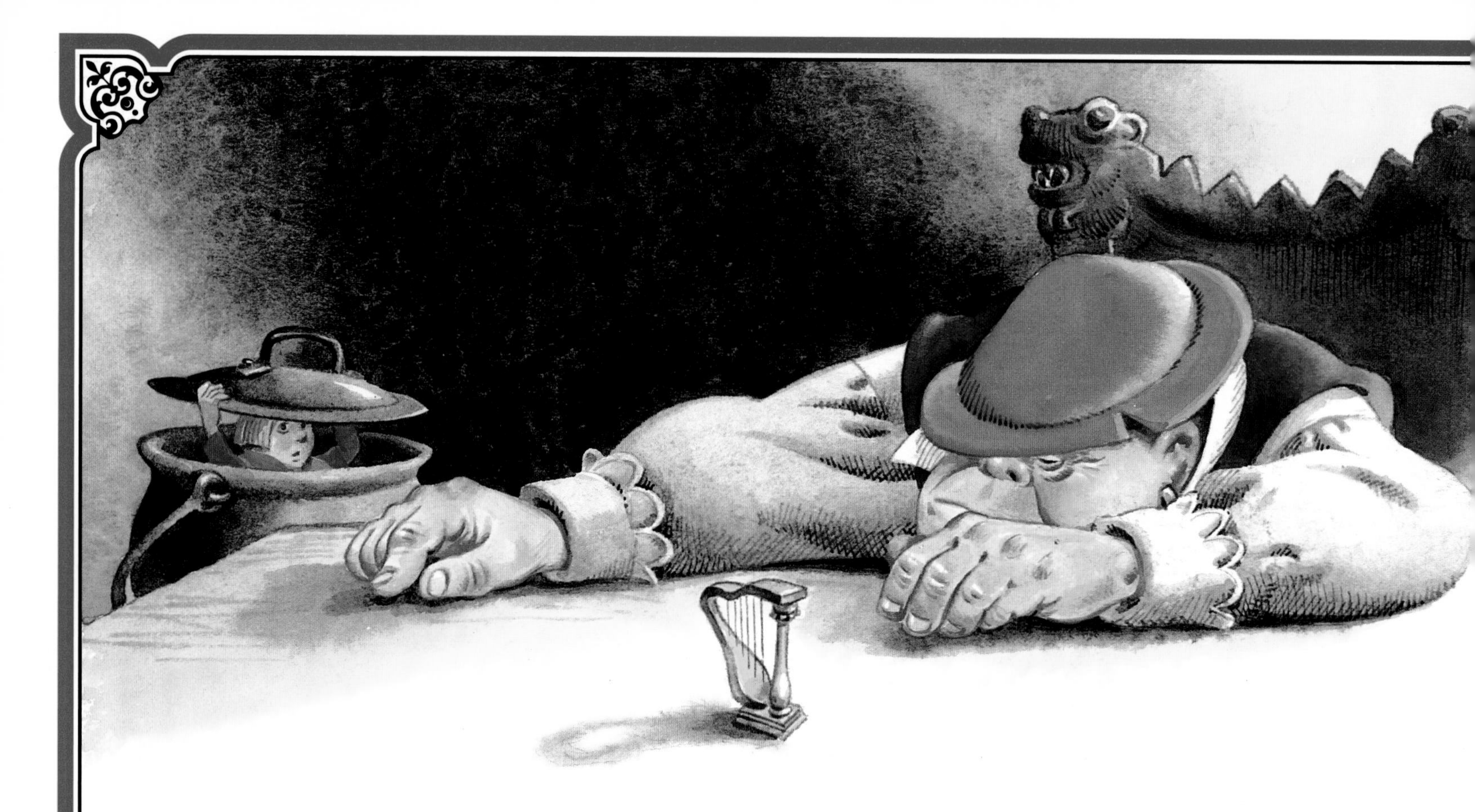

“Is that all you stole? A hen?” she asked Jack, disappointed.
“Just wait,” he said to his mother. A little while later the hen laid a golden egg. In fact, it laid a golden egg every single day after that. By now, Jack and his mother were very wealthy. They hired carpenters to completely rebuild their house and they furnished it with many beautiful things. Their old shack was transformed into a luxurious home.
Jack and his mother had not forgotten their years of poverty. So they welcomed any traveler who needed food or shelter. But wealth doesn’t always bring happiness. Jack’s mother suddenly fell ill. Not one of the many doctors who visited her could discover what her illness was. The woman was sad, ate less and less, and showed no interest in life. She rarely smiled, and then only when Jack was near her. Her son tried to cheer her up.
Jack was desperate and didn’t know what to do. All the hen’s gold was not enough to make his mother well again. So, one day, he had another idea.

"What if I went back to the ogre's castle? Maybe there I could find the answer," he thought.
One evening he gathered all his courage and climbed the giant beanstalk once more. This time he entered the castle through an open window. He sneaked into the kitchen and hid inside a huge pot. After dinner the ogre went to get his magic harp. While listening to the harp's sweet melody, the ogre fell asleep. In his hiding place, Jack was captivated as well by the harp's song. When he finally heard the ogre snore loudly, he quickly climbed on the table and ran away with the harp in his hands. The instrument woke up the ogre screaming,
"Master, master! Wake up! A thief is taking me away!"
The ogre woke up suddenly and began chasing Jack. The boy ran away as fast as he could.
He finally arrived at the beanstalk and quickly slid down.
When Jack got down to earth he called to his mother,
"Look what I've brought you!"

The harp began to play an enchanting melody. But Jack soon realized with terror that the beanstalk was shaking. The ogre was coming down to earth! "Hide the harp and bring me an ax! I must chop down the beanstalk," Jack said to his mother. They could already see the ogre's huge boots when the stalk and the ogre finally crashed to the ground. The ogre fell down a nearby cliff, never to be seen again.

The magical sound of the harp cured his mother's sadness. The hen kept on laying golden eggs. Jack's life had gone through many changes since he had accepted the magic beans. But thanks to his courage and wit, he and his mother found happiness, and lived a good life.

Gulliver's Travels

Once upon a time . . . there was an English doctor named Gulliver. A very amazing adventure befell him when he boarded the ship *Antilope* at Bristol, directed toward the East Indies. During a strong storm he was tossed overboard, and the ship sunk. Gulliver hung on to a plank of wood, and fought the waves during the long night. By morning the sea had finally calmed and the doctor was carried by the current toward a deserted beach. Exhausted, he fell into a deep sleep.

The sun was high in the sky when Gulliver woke up. He squinted and tried to raise his arm to cover his face, but he could not move his hand. He could not move his other arm, either. He tried to raise his head and realized that his hair was tied to the ground. His legs were stuck as well. Gulliver could hear a humming confusion around him, but he could only see the sky and could not understand what was happening. Suddenly he felt something crawl up his leg and across

his chest until it reached his chin. Gulliver tried to look down. With surprise, he realized that on his chest stood a very little man. He was about six inches tall and was armed with bow and arrows.

Gulliver was able to free his right arm, and he turned on his side. He realized that a large army of these very small men had tied him to the ground with rope. He picked up the little man standing in front of him, and freeing the other arm, he tried to explain that he was very thirsty. The little man whistled sharply, and soon carts arrived carrying vats filled with beverages. Gulliver drank more than fifty of these, and he also ate some rolls that were the size of buckshot.
All the while, Gulliver held on to the little man who seemed to be in charge, as a kind of hostage.

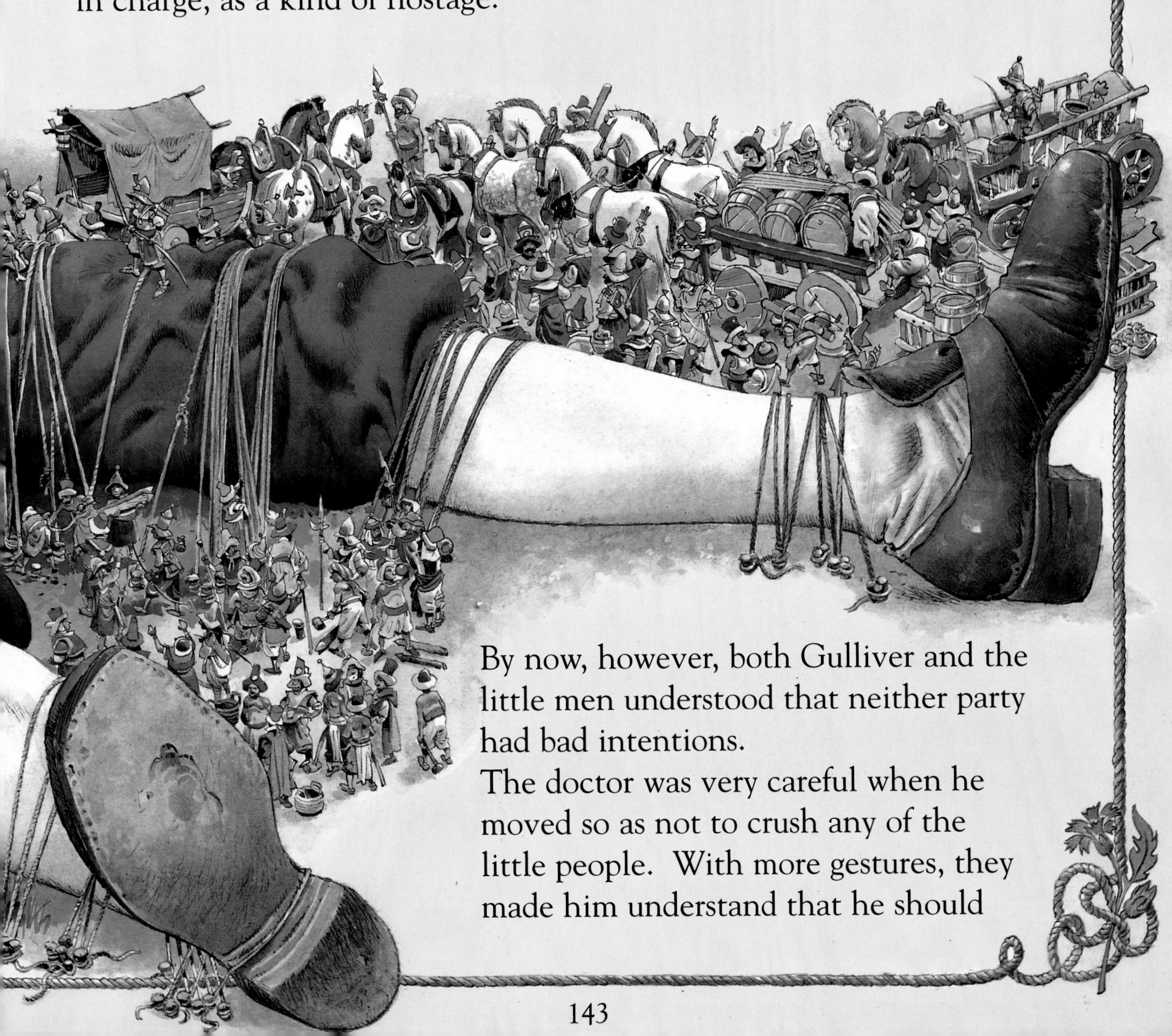

By now, however, both Gulliver and the little men understood that neither party had bad intentions.
The doctor was very careful when he moved so as not to crush any of the little people. With more gestures, they made him understand that he should

get up and follow them.
The country that Gulliver saw was all in miniature. The trees, the rivers — everything was proportionately sized. They soon reached the city; Gulliver was brought to a tower where some important people had gathered. Among these was the emperor.

They spoke with a great megaphone, and Gulliver heard the word "Lilliput" more than once. He realized that this was the name of the strange place where he had landed.
Next to the tower there was a large building, and it was indicated to Gulliver that he should stay there.
The doctor allowed the little people to chain one of his feet, although he knew that he would be able to free himself, if necessary.

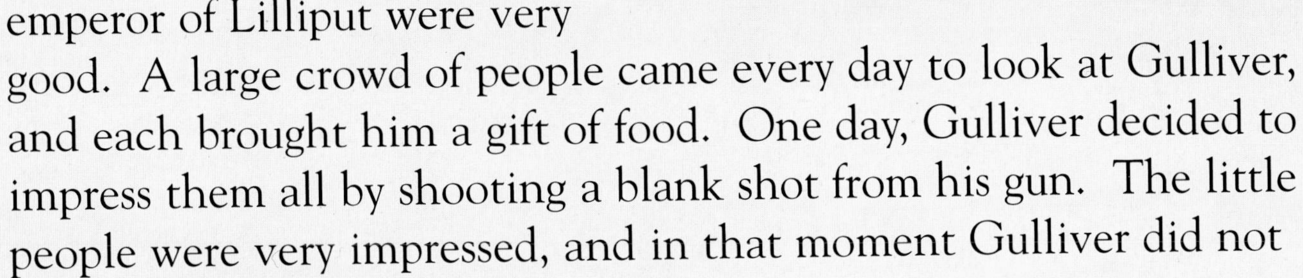

The Lilliputians brought him all kinds of food. Slowly, they learned to communicate. The doctor's relations with the emperor of Lilliput were very good. A large crowd of people came every day to look at Gulliver, and each brought him a gift of food. One day, Gulliver decided to impress them all by shooting a blank shot from his gun. The little people were very impressed, and in that moment Gulliver did not realize that he had changed his destiny.

From the shipwreck Gulliver had saved his sword, a pistol, his watch, his diary, a razor, a few coins, and an old comb. The emperor wanted to know exactly how Gulliver used each of these objects.

The emperor was especially interested when he saw how, with just one swipe of his sword, Gulliver could quickly cut down an entire cluster of trees.

Gulliver learned quite a bit about the culture of the Lilliputians. He understood why many of them were very often armed.

Beyond the seas there was an island called Blefuscu, whose inhabitants were the enemies of the Lilliputians, and had been for a long time. One day, one of the emperor's messengers arrived, asking Gulliver to come as quickly as possible to the palace. Naturally, Gulliver awaited the emperor in the courtyard, since he could not enter the palace itself. The emperor explained that a war was about to begin. His spies had informed him that the battleships of Blefuscu were ready to invade the island of Lilliput. The emperor asked Gulliver if he were willing to help the Lilliputians. Gulliver accepted on two conditions:

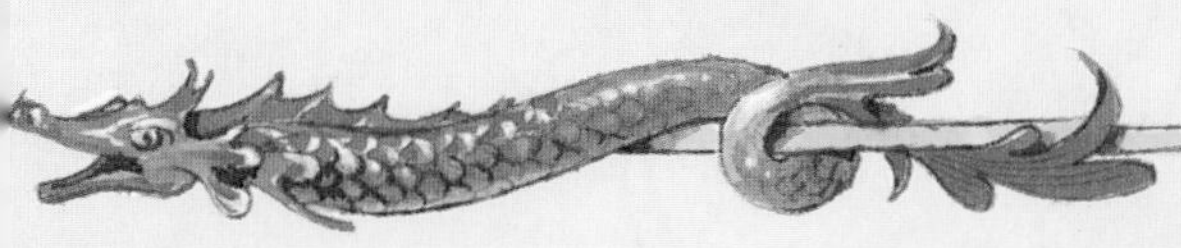

one, that there should be no victims; and two, should the Lilliputians win, the emperor was to help Gulliver to return to the world from which he had come.

Naturally the emperor accepted Gulliver's conditions.

In preparation, Gulliver requested that the depth of the water be measured all around the island. When he learned that the water reached only to his waistline, he began to prepare a plan of attack. He waited for a very dense fog on the sea, and walking through the water he reached the port of Blefuscu. Here, to the surprise of the islanders, he broke the moorings of the boats, and pulling them out to sea, he sunk them. Lilliput was safe!

Gulliver was quite certain that he had resolved his problems, but he did not know that the emperor would not keep his promise.
As a gift the emperor gave him a black hat that he had commissioned, made by twenty-four tailors.
The emperor, however, would not assist Gulliver in leaving Lilliput. Gulliver was too precious to the emperor . . .

. . . who wanted to take over Blefuscu. The commander told him, “If you do not follow the emperor’s wishes, he will have you poisoned!” Gulliver was afraid. Poison was a weapon against which he could not defend himself. So he decided to escape. One night he loaded all of his belongings onto a ship and pulled it behind him across the sea to Blefuscu. When he arrived, he asked to speak to the king.

He explained, "As long as I am here, Lilliput can never attack you! In exchange, help me to return to my country." Gulliver was welcome in Blefuscu, and whenever he asked for assistance, all were ready and willing to help him.
To begin, Gulliver inspected the coasts of the island, and looked for any shipwrecked boats that might have washed up in the night.
In fact, he soon found the hull of a boat washed ashore.
He realized that with a lot of work he might be able to repair it.
It took many months, but finally the great day arrived.
For a week the inhabitants of Blefuscu brought food and water

onto the boat. Gulliver was finally ready to depart. After a few days, Blefuscu was just a tiny dot on the horizon. For days and days Gulliver rowed, until he realized that a strong current was pushing the boat forward. In the meantime, a strange and heavy fog had descended on the sea. When the fog suddenly lifted, Gulliver saw seagulls flying overhead. To his joy, he realized that they were normal-size seagulls, not the miniature gulls he had seen in Lilliput. Gulliver had finally returned to his world.

The Pied Piper of Hamelin

Once upon a time . . . on the banks of a great river in the north of Germany lay a town called Hamelin. The citizens were honest folk who lived contentedly at first. The years went by, and the town grew rich. Then one day an extraordinary thing happened. Rats had never been a danger in Hamelin, because the cats had always managed to catch them. Now, all at once, the rats began to multiply. Soon a black sea of rats swarmed over the town. They attacked the barns and storehouses, and then ran into the houses and chewed on anything they could find.

The terrified citizens flocked to the town hall and demanded that the Mayor and councilors do something.

"More cats!" someone shouted. But all the cats had fled.

"We must get help," said the Mayor solemnly. But he had no idea where to find it. Just then there came a loud knock at the door. The councilors opened it. To their surprise, a tall, thin man dressed in brightly colored clothes walked in, carrying a long, golden pipe.

"I am the Pied Piper," announced the stranger. "I've freed other towns of beetles and bats. And for a thousand florins I'll rid you of all your rats."

"A thousand florins!" cried the mayor. "We'll give you *fifty thousand* if you succeed!"

"A thousand will do," said the stranger quietly. "By sunrise tomorrow there won't be a rat left in Hamelin."

In the gray light before dawn, the sweet sound of a pipe echoed through the town. The Pied Piper walked slowly along the streets.

Out from the doors and windows came the rats, scrambling and squeaking in their hurry to follow the music.
The Pied Piper walked through every street in town. Then, with an army of rats scampering behind him, he turned and walked toward the river.
Right into the river he walked, and stood knee-deep in the fast-flowing water. The rats swarmed after him, only to be swept away and drowned. By the time the sun rose, there wasn't a rat left!
The people cheered and the town councilors rubbed their hands in glee at finding such an easy way out of their trouble. Soon, however, there came a knock on the councilors' door.

"My one thousand florins," said the Pied Piper.

"Ah, yes," replied the Mayor grandly. "Well, my good man, the rats are all dead now. It really wasn't much work, and I think you should be satisfied with fifty florins."

"A thousand florins, or you'll be sorry!" said the Piper angrily.

The Mayor shook his head. "Fifty or nothing."

"Broken promises lead to broken hearts," warned the Pied Piper, and he vanished. That night the citizens of Hamelin slept soundly for the first time in weeks.

When the strange sound of piping wafted through the streets at dawn, only the children heard it. Drawn by the sweet music, they crept out of their houses.

Soon a long procession of children was following the Piper. Last in line was a lame boy, hobbling along with a crutch.

The Piper left the town and walked toward the foot of a big, rocky mountain. When he came close, he played his pipe more sweetly than ever, and a huge rock rolled away, revealing a door.

What wonderful things the children saw inside the mountain! They hurried past the rock after the Piper. The lame boy, far behind, could see a marvelous cave and shimmering lights. "Wait for me!" he called. But he was too slow, and the great rock rolled back into place. When the townspeople awoke to find all their children gone, they searched everywhere.

At last they came upon the lame boy, who told them what happened. "We were too greedy," said the town councilors sadly, mindful of the Pied Piper's warning.

The children were never heard from again; but it is said that far away, in a land beyond the great mountain, lives a tribe of happy people whose legends say they are descended from the lost children of Hamelin.

The Gnome's Red Scarf

Once upon a time . . . there was a very ingenious gnome. His job was to buy old paintings, pots and pans, trunks, and literally anything that was not needed anymore. The gnome was a very small fellow, however, and he had to move very heavy objects with his cart. All night long he would stay awake and work on an old project of his: the steam-powered cart. After many, many attempts, he was finally able to build it. The steam-powered cart worked, and so to celebrate, a great party was planned.

After the celebrations, the gnome left to do some business in a city that he had never been to before. Business was very good, and for next to nothing he was able to buy an enormous quantity of old things, and he loaded them all onto his cart. He had never been so satisfied in his entire lifetime! But on the way home . . .

. . . the troubles began. On a dark night, in a furious storm of sleet and snow, he lost his way. Suddenly, there was a great splash and the cart fell into a pond.

The gnome was cold and he was also afraid. He stayed there all night with a scarf wrapped around his neck, waiting for the morning. At dawn a great fog had covered the pond.
The gnome sat and waited for someone to pass by.

He heard croaking, which grew louder and louder, and slowly the fog lifted to reveal: frogs! They were everywhere, left, right, in the water, and on the banks of the pond. He was surrounded by frogs. Then there was a great confusion and the King of the Frogs arrived. When he appeared, all of the other frogs fell silent.

"What are you doing in my kingdom?" asked the king.

The gnome, who was frightened, responded, "Your Majesty, last night I fell into the pond!"

"I can see that! But no one should enter the pond without my permission. This is not good! Not good at all!" said the king. "What nice things do you have in your cart?"

"Oh, many old things that really have no value," answered the gnome as he opened the door of the cart.

The King of the Frogs, who had just recently built a house in the reeds, had an idea.
"If you want I can help you to pull your cart out of the pond, but in exchange you must give me the contents of the cart!" Then he rubbed his hands contentedly. With all of those beautiful things the king could furnish his house like a palace! The gnome almost began to cry at the thought of losing everything he had bought on his trip! But he had an idea, and so he said to the king, "All right your Majesty, I will give you everything. Be kind, though, and at least let me keep the few things that will fit into the wool of my poor red scarf." The king clapped his hands.
"I accept! King's honor!" Then he shouted his orders.

In marched the frogs of the royal guard. A general commanded the operations, but the frogs were not strong enough to pull the cart out of the water. The help of a beaver and two water rats was needed. Finally the cart was dried off completely. Everyone was very excited. In the meantime, the gnome went into the cart and took off his scarf.

He then began to unravel a long piece of wool. He wrapped the long piece of wool around and around the cart.
The king, who had been advised that the cart was out of the pond, reappeared. The gnome reminded him, "King's honor! You said that all that would fit into the wool of my scarf would remain mine! Unfortunately, there is nothing left for you, your Majesty!" The King of the Frogs realized that he had been tricked. He could do

nothing but keep his word. So he stood up and said, "The king's word is sacred!" The gnome, so happy to have all of his goods, gave everything to his friends. "I would rather give all of this to you than to the King of the Frogs!" he said happily to the black bear, handing him a jar. "It is the best honey I could find!" Then he turned to his friends and said, "In exchange you can make me a new red scarf!"

*A*ESOP'S *F*ABLES

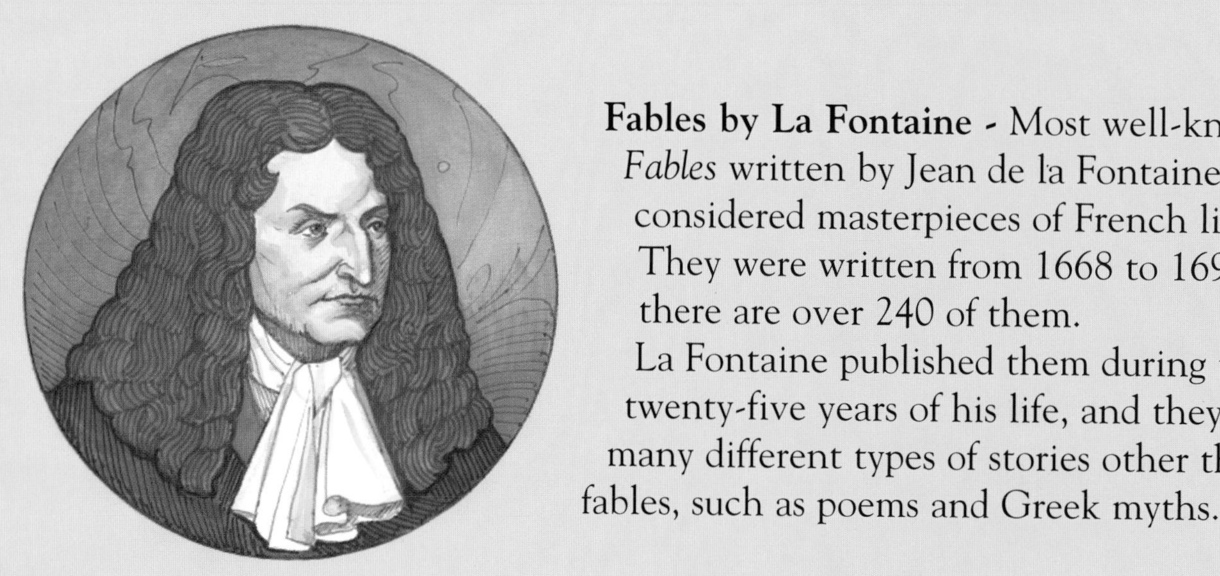

Fables by La Fontaine - Most well-known are the *Fables* written by Jean de la Fontaine. They are considered masterpieces of French literature. They were written from 1668 to 1694, and there are over 240 of them.

La Fontaine published them during the last twenty-five years of his life, and they include many different types of stories other than animal fables, such as poems and Greek myths.

Paris . . . in the 1600s was an important place for the development of literature. La Fontaine was not born in Paris, but he moved there and it was in Paris that he met many very important people. He was supported by important members of the government, by wealthy noblewomen, and he participated in salons, where writers, philosophers and other intellectuals gathered to discuss topics of culture. Like many other distinguished French writers (including Charles Perrault), La Fontaine was elected to the Académie Française.

Above, Jean de la Fontaine was born in 1621. He died in 1695 in Paris, France.

At right, an officer of the French king, Louis XIV, on horseback, with his attendant.

Did Aesop Really Exist? - Some believe that Aesop lived in the 6th century B.C., but no one really knows for sure. It is known that a collection of animal fables came to be known as "Aesop's fables," and these stories have influenced many writers since then, among these Jean de la Fontaine (pictured at far left) who wrote in the 17th century in France. Nowadays, Aesop is legendary and the animal fables are known all over the world.

Above, a bust of the supposed figure of Aesop, fashioned by the Greek sculptor Lysippus, who lived from approximately 360 to 316 B.C.

Phaedrus . . . writing in the time of the Roman emperor Augustus, also collected many animal fables (and added some of his own as well); he also influenced La Fontaine. In the fables, animals speak and act like human beings, and many fables have a moral, demonstrating for the reader the difference between right and wrong.

Above, "The Fox and the Grapes."

Left, a play by the French writer, Molière, and a noblewoman in her sedan-chair in France, circa 1670.

The Hare and the Tortoise

Once upon a time . . . there was a boastful hare who was forever teasing a tortoise for its slowness. One day the irate tortoise answered back, “Who do you think you are, anyway? You may be swift, but even you can be beaten!”

The hare squealed with laughter. “Not by you, surely! I bet nobody can win against me. Care to try?”

Annoyed by such bragging, the tortoise accepted the challenge. A course was planned, and the next day at dawn they stood at the starting line.

The hare yawned lazily as the tortoise trudged off. “Take your time,” he said. “I’ll have forty winks and catch up with you in a minute.”

A little later the hare woke with a start and looked

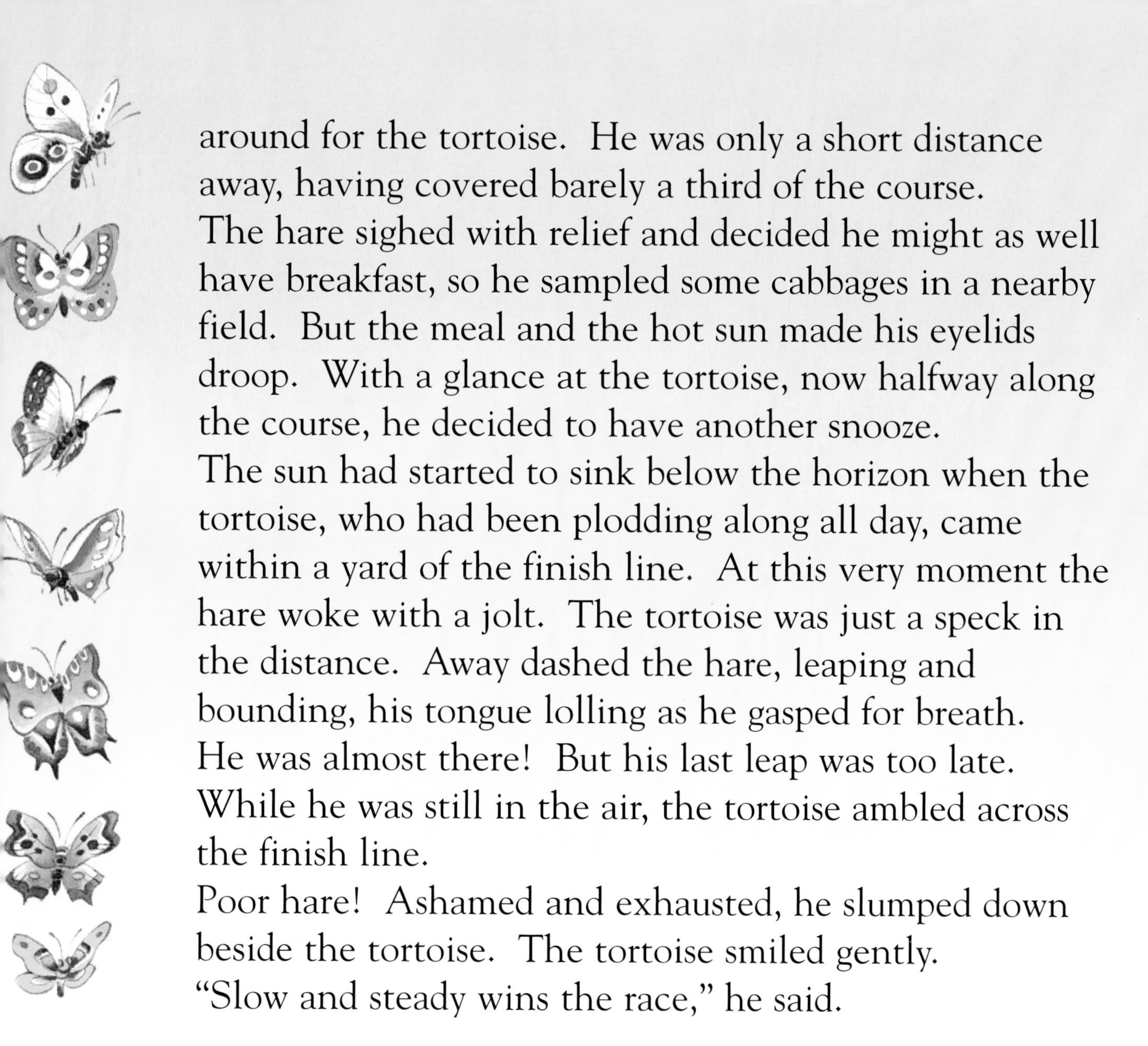

around for the tortoise. He was only a short distance away, having covered barely a third of the course.
The hare sighed with relief and decided he might as well have breakfast, so he sampled some cabbages in a nearby field. But the meal and the hot sun made his eyelids droop. With a glance at the tortoise, now halfway along the course, he decided to have another snooze.
The sun had started to sink below the horizon when the tortoise, who had been plodding along all day, came within a yard of the finish line. At this very moment the hare woke with a jolt. The tortoise was just a speck in the distance. Away dashed the hare, leaping and bounding, his tongue lolling as he gasped for breath.
He was almost there! But his last leap was too late.
While he was still in the air, the tortoise ambled across the finish line.
Poor hare! Ashamed and exhausted, he slumped down beside the tortoise. The tortoise smiled gently.
"Slow and steady wins the race," he said.

The Country Mouse and the Town Mouse

Once upon a time . . . a town mouse, on a trip to the country, met a country mouse. They spent the day together and became friends. The country mouse took his new friend into the meadows, letting him sample all the good things of the land. The town mouse was thrilled, and to thank his friend, he invited the country mouse to visit him in town.

When the country mouse saw his friend's pantry, full of hams, cheese, honey, jam, and other goodies, he was amazed.

"I've never seen anything like it! Are all these wonderful things for eating?" "Of course!" came the reply. "You're my guest — help yourself!"
They began to eat. The country mouse tried not to stuff himself. He wanted to taste everything!

“You’re the luckiest mouse I’ve ever met!” said the country mouse. The town mouse was listening to his friend’s praise, when the sound of footsteps interrupted their feast.
“Run!” whispered the town mouse to his friend.
They were just in time: there stood the lady of the house! What a fright!

Luckily, she went away and the two mice returned to enjoy their meal.
“It’s all right!” said the town mouse. “She’s gone. How about some honey? It’s delicious!” Tasting it, the country mouse exclaimed, “Yummy! I’ve never eaten anything so good in my life!”
Suddenly, there came the sound of footsteps again!

It was the man of the house. When he saw the spilt honey, he groaned, “Those mice! I’ll send the cat!” Trembling, the mice hid. They held their breath, not making a sound.
When all was quiet again, they got up the courage to leave.
“We can come out! There’s nobody here!” the town mouse whispered.
Suddenly, the pantry door creaked.

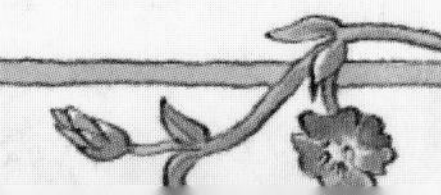

The two mice froze with fear.
A pair of yellow eyes glowed in the dark. A large cat was in the pantry! The two mice tiptoed silently back to their hole.
As luck would have it, the cat discovered a juicy sausage.
He stopped to eat it, and no longer hungry, decided to leave mouse-hunting for another day.
Now, the country mouse did not lose a second. He shook hands with his friend, saying,
"Thanks so much! But I must rush off! I'd much rather sit down to a simple meal in peace, in the country, than have a spread of delicious food, surrounded by danger on all sides!"

THE FOX AND THE CROW

Once upon a time . . . a big crow stole a piece of cheese and went to perch on a branch to eat it in peace. A passing fox sniffed the air and stopped below the tree, his mouth watering. "Cheese?" he said. "Mmm, I would love some . . . ," he said to himself greedily, wondering how to get hold of the morsel. After a moment he spoke to the crow. "You are a fine crow! I have never seen one so big and strong. What thick and shiny feathers you have! And slender legs, the sign of a noble bird. And a regal beak. That is it: the beak of a king! You ought to be crowned King of the Birds!" When the crow heard such praise of his beauty, he stretched to his full length and triumphantly flapped his wings. In his softest voice the fox went on. "What lovely eyes you

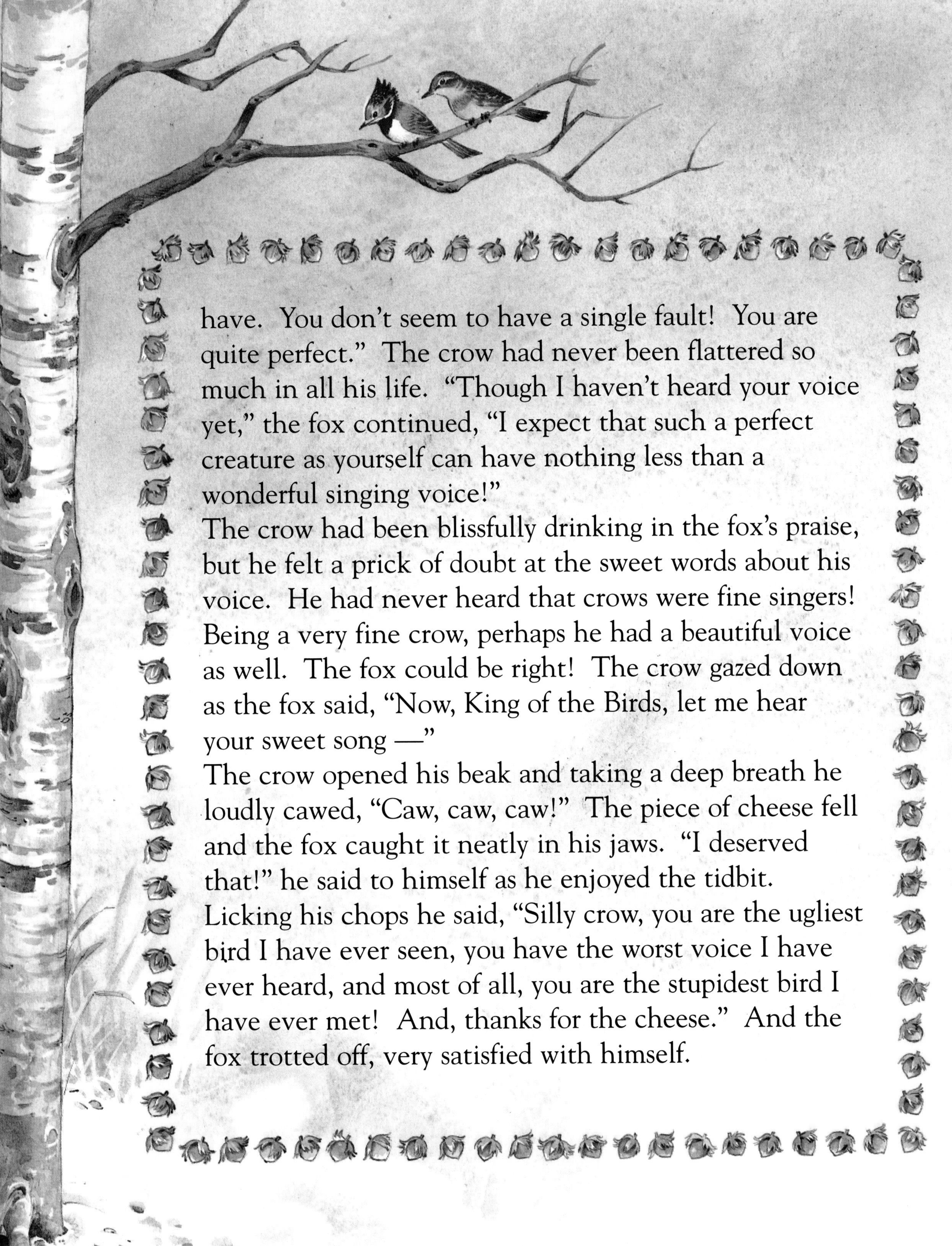

have. You don't seem to have a single fault! You are quite perfect." The crow had never been flattered so much in all his life. "Though I haven't heard your voice yet," the fox continued, "I expect that such a perfect creature as yourself can have nothing less than a wonderful singing voice!"

The crow had been blissfully drinking in the fox's praise, but he felt a prick of doubt at the sweet words about his voice. He had never heard that crows were fine singers! Being a very fine crow, perhaps he had a beautiful voice as well. The fox could be right! The crow gazed down as the fox said, "Now, King of the Birds, let me hear your sweet song —"

The crow opened his beak and taking a deep breath he loudly cawed, "Caw, caw, caw!" The piece of cheese fell and the fox caught it neatly in his jaws. "I deserved that!" he said to himself as he enjoyed the tidbit.

Licking his chops he said, "Silly crow, you are the ugliest bird I have ever seen, you have the worst voice I have ever heard, and most of all, you are the stupidest bird I have ever met! And, thanks for the cheese." And the fox trotted off, very satisfied with himself.

The Ant and the Cricket

Once upon a time . . . on a hot summer afternoon a cricket sang cheerfully on the branch of a tree, while down below, a long line of ants struggled gamely under the weight of their load of grains. Between one song and the next, the cricket spoke to the

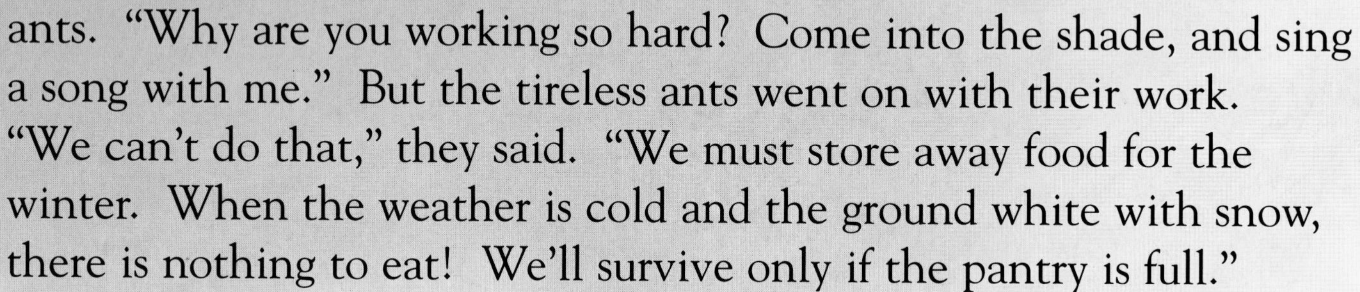

ants. "Why are you working so hard? Come into the shade, and sing a song with me." But the tireless ants went on with their work. "We can't do that," they said. "We must store away food for the winter. When the weather is cold and the ground white with snow, there is nothing to eat! We'll survive only if the pantry is full."

"There's plenty of summer to come," replied the cricket, "and lots of time to fill the pantry. I'd rather sing! How can anyone work in this heat?"

All summer the cricket sang while the ants labored. But the days turned into weeks and the weeks into months. Autumn came, the leaves began to fall, and the cricket left the bare tree. The grass too was turning thin and yellow.

One morning, the cricket woke shivering with cold. An early frost had tinged the fields with white and turned the last of the green leaves brown: winter had come at last. The cricket wandered, feeding on the few dry stalks left on the hard frozen ground. Then the snow fell and he could find nothing to eat at all. Trembling and famished the cricket thought sadly of the warmth and his summer songs. One evening, he saw a speck of light in the distance, and went toward it.

"Please open the door! I'm starving! Give me some food!" said the cricket. An ant leaned out of the window. "Who's there? Who is it?"

"It is I — the cricket. I'm cold and hungry, with no roof over my head," replied the cricket.

"The cricket? I remember you. And what were you doing all summer while we were getting ready for winter?"

"Me? I was singing and filling the whole earth and sky with my song!"

"Singing, eh?" said the ant. "Well, try dancing now!"

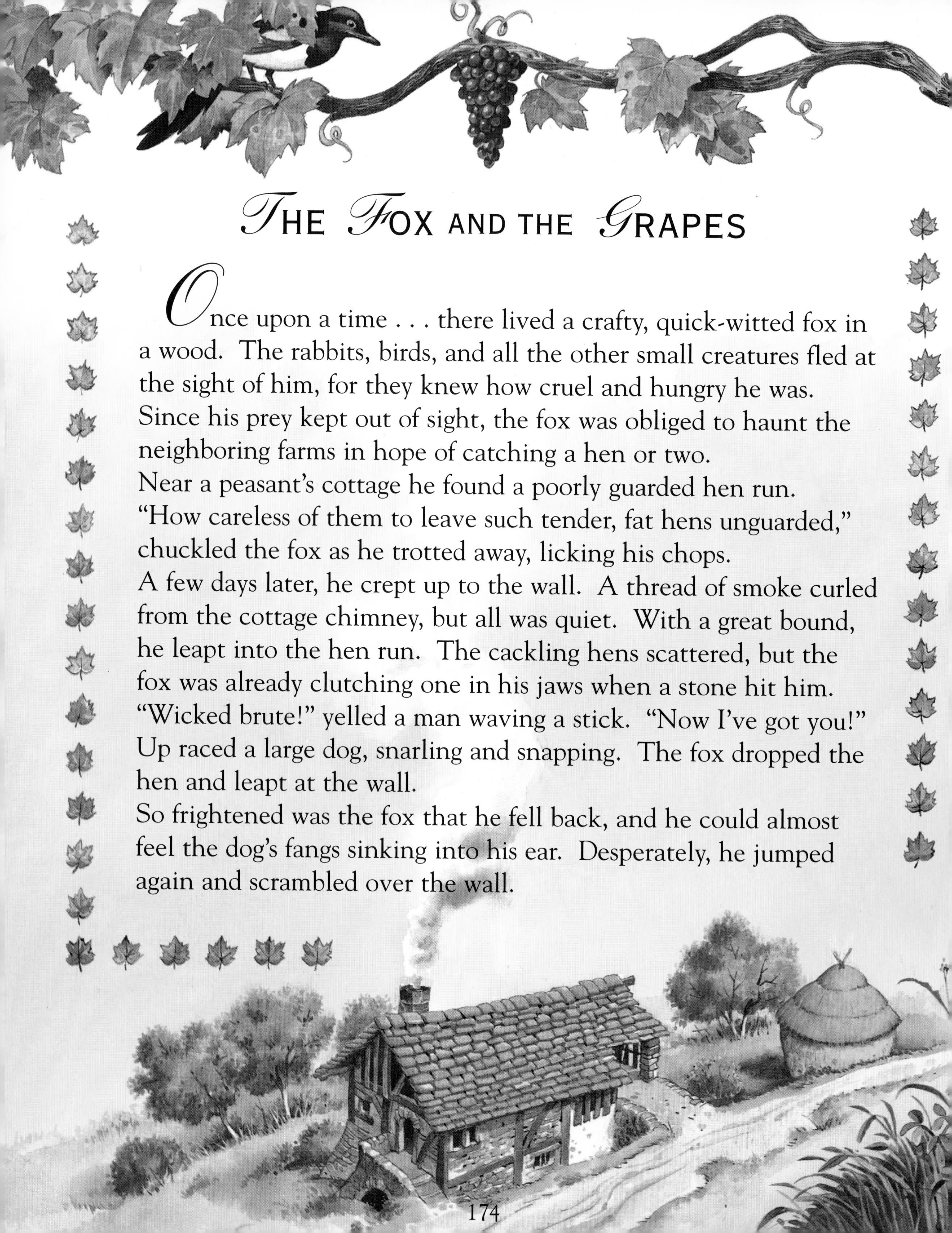

The Fox and the Grapes

Once upon a time . . . there lived a crafty, quick-witted fox in a wood. The rabbits, birds, and all the other small creatures fled at the sight of him, for they knew how cruel and hungry he was. Since his prey kept out of sight, the fox was obliged to haunt the neighboring farms in hope of catching a hen or two.

Near a peasant's cottage he found a poorly guarded hen run.

"How careless of them to leave such tender, fat hens unguarded," chuckled the fox as he trotted away, licking his chops.

A few days later, he crept up to the wall. A thread of smoke curled from the cottage chimney, but all was quiet. With a great bound, he leapt into the hen run. The cackling hens scattered, but the fox was already clutching one in his jaws when a stone hit him.

"Wicked brute!" yelled a man waving a stick. "Now I've got you!"

Up raced a large dog, snarling and snapping. The fox dropped the hen and leapt at the wall.

So frightened was the fox that he fell back, and he could almost feel the dog's fangs sinking into his ear. Desperately, he jumped again and scrambled over the wall.

He raced away, followed by shouts.
"Bad luck!" he muttered, but hunger gnawed at his stomach, and he looked around for another meal.
Right above his head was a vine, laden with bunches of ripe grapes.
"Well, if there's nothing else . . . ," he said, and jumped at the grapes. But the fruit was hanging just beyond his reach.
The fox took a running jump, but without success. Over and over he tried, but the grapes always remained beyond his grasp.
"Caw! Caw! Caw!" mocked a passing crow overhead.
"Ha!" retorted the fox, with disgust.
"They're sour grapes anyway. Who wants to eat them? I'll come back when they're ripe." And he marched off, his stomach empty and his chest thrust out with pride.

The Vain Crow

Once upon a time . . . a restless crow decided to go farther away than usual from home and friends. In a farmyard, he met a pair of peacocks. What beautiful birds they were! The crow had never seen such beautiful feathers, and he timidly asked the regal-looking birds what they were. "We are peacocks," one of them replied, spreading his tail. As the peacock strutted about showing his magnificent feathers, he screamed, as peacocks do. Bursting with admiration, the crow said goodbye and flapped away, but as he flew home he could not forget the two peacocks. "What fine feathers! They must be so happy, being so beautiful." He gazed down at his own ugly plumes. From that day on, he could not help thinking about the splendor of the peacocks. He even stopped looking at himself

in the pond water, for every time he did so, it made him more depressed. He spied on the peacocks, and the more he watched them strut around, the more envious he was of their beauty. One day, he noticed that one of the peacocks had dropped a feather. When the sun went down, the crow picked it up and hid it away. For days on end, he watched the peacocks and found more feathers. When he had four, he could wait no longer: he stuck the peacock feathers onto his own tail, and started to parade about in front of his friends. "Just look at my gorgeous tail!" he said proudly. "I'm not ugly like you! Out of my way, you moth-eaten crows!" The crows' amazement soon changed to indignation, then they started to laugh at their vain companion. "You are nothing but a crow yourself, even with those flashy feathers!"

"And you are silly as well as ugly," replied the crow haughtily, and off he went to live with the peacocks.

When the peacocks set eyes on the stranger, they thought the crow was just another peacock who, for some reason, had lost most of his feathers and they felt sorry for him. But the crow, vainer than ever, wanted to attract admiration and a foolish idea came into his head. He tried to scream the way peacocks do. But the harsh "Caw! Caw! Caw!" quickly betrayed the crow. The furious peacocks pecked the stolen feathers off and chased the crow away. Poor crow! For when, sad and downcast, he went back to his friends, he was given exactly the same treatment. Nobody would speak to him and all the crows turned their backs on him for trying to be what he was not.

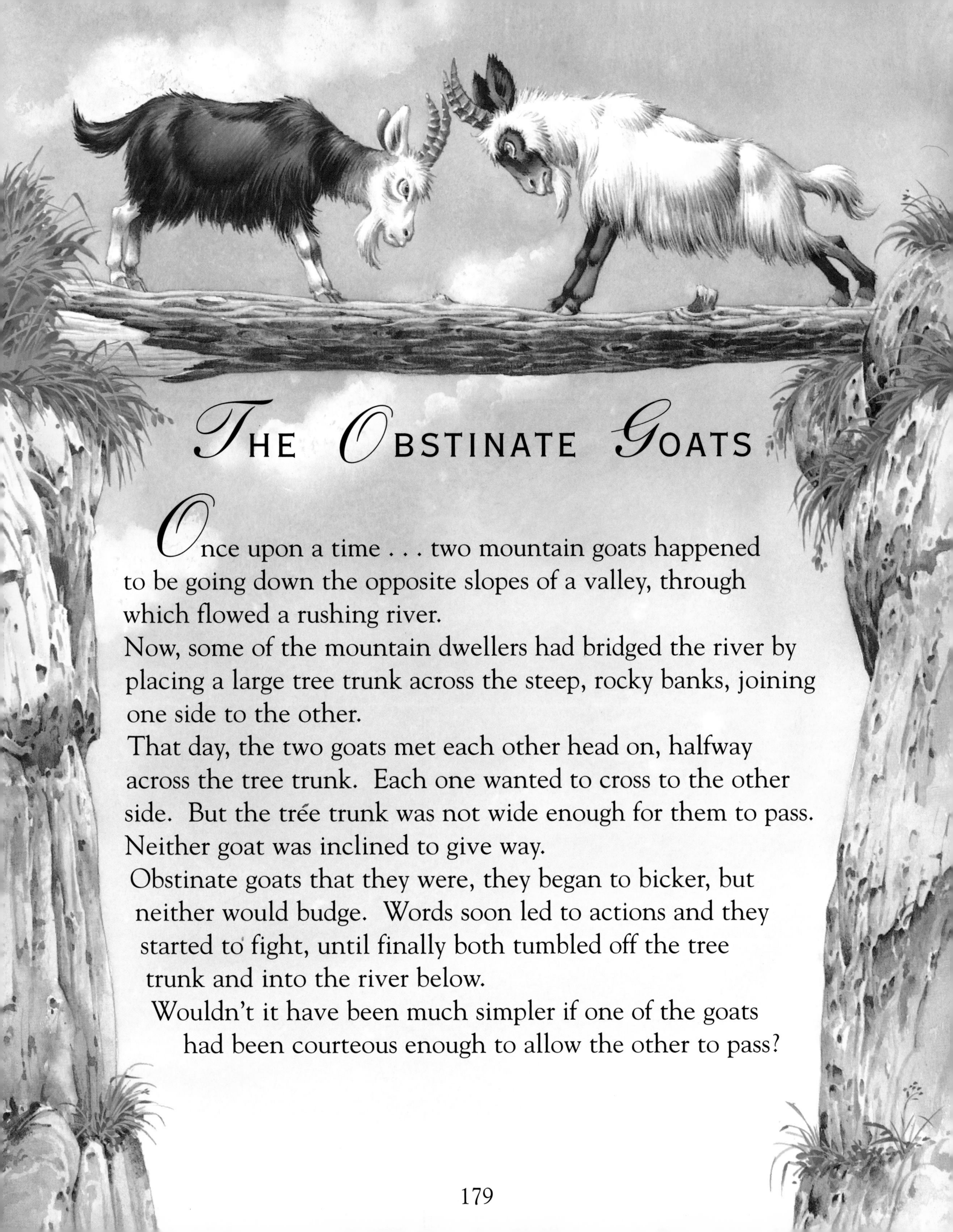

The Obstinate Goats

Once upon a time . . . two mountain goats happened to be going down the opposite slopes of a valley, through which flowed a rushing river.

Now, some of the mountain dwellers had bridged the river by placing a large tree trunk across the steep, rocky banks, joining one side to the other.

That day, the two goats met each other head on, halfway across the tree trunk. Each one wanted to cross to the other side. But the tree trunk was not wide enough for them to pass. Neither goat was inclined to give way.

Obstinate goats that they were, they began to bicker, but neither would budge. Words soon led to actions and they started to fight, until finally both tumbled off the tree trunk and into the river below.

Wouldn't it have been much simpler if one of the goats had been courteous enough to allow the other to pass?

The Ox and the Frog

Once upon a time . . . there was a conceited frog who never passed up a chance to show how much better than everyone else he was. He always tried to jump the highest, and when it came to diving, he was first into the water. He had to be first all the time. One day, a big ox came to drink at the pond. Frightened, all the frogs hopped away, but when they saw that the ox was harmless, they came out again. "Isn't he enormous!" they exclaimed to one another.

One frog said, "It would take hundreds of frogs to make one of him!" Listening to his friends' remarks, the conceited frog said, "He's certainly bigger than we are. But he's not enormous!" And puffing out his chest he announced, "I could easily become as big as that ox! Look!" "You're far too little!" they said. But the frog just puffed himself out even more. "Now look!" he whispered, trying not to lose air. His friends giggled. "What about now?" he gasped, as he puffed himself up some more. "The ox is still much bigger," came the reply. The conceited frog made a last great effort: taking an extra deep breath, he puffed himself up until . . . BANG! His skin burst! Nothing was left of the conceited frog but scraps of green skin.

The ox went back to his drinking, and the frogs hopped away, remarking, "It just doesn't do to become too swollen-headed."

The Fox and the Stork

Once upon a time . . . a fox made friends with a stork and invited her to lunch. Wondering what to serve, he thought he would play a trick on the bird. He prepared a tasty soup and poured it into two flat plates. "Help yourself, Mrs. Stork! It is frog soup and chopped parsley. Taste it, it is very good!"

"Thank you very much!" said the stork, sniffing the soup. But quickly she saw that the fox had played a trick on her. For no matter how she tried, she could not drink from the flat plate. The fox urged her on, saying, "Eat up! Do you like it?" But all the stork could do was bluff. With a casual air she replied, "I have such a headache that I have lost my appetite!" And the fox replied, "What a shame! It is a good soup. Next time —"

To which the stork quickly replied, “Yes! Next time, you must have lunch with me!” The very next day, the fox found a polite invitation on his front door. “Now isn’t that nice?” said the fox to himself, “And she hasn’t taken my little trick to heart!” The stork’s house was much plainer than the fox’s, and she apologized. “My home is much humbler than yours,” she said, “but I’ve cooked a special meal. Freshwater shrimp with white wine and juniper berries!” The fox licked his chops when the stork handed him his jar. But, try as he might, he was unable to reach down into the neck of the jar. With her long beak, the stork ate easily. “Try it!” she said. “Do you like it?” But the fox, confused and outsmarted, could not think of anything to say. As he tossed and turned hungrily in bed that night, he said to himself with a sigh, “I might have known!”

The Wolf and the Lamb

Once upon a time . . . in the forest lived a wolf, known to be savage and ruthless. One day, feeling thirsty, the wolf went down to a stream, and as he drank the sparkling water, he saw a lamb drinking further downstream. The minute he set eyes on the lamb, he decided to make a meal of it. “A nice plump lamb! That will be delicious! I haven’t had such luck in ages! Now, I must find an excuse to quarrel, so that no one can accuse me of gobbling it down unjustly!”

Unaware of the wolf, the lamb was happily sipping the water when it heard a deep growl. "You down there! You are muddying my drinking water!" The lamb gasped in surprise. "I am sorry Mr. Wolf, but it cannot possibly be so. I am below you, and the water is flowing downhill, not up!"
The wicked wolf was taken aback, but only for an instant. He quickly found another excuse to be angry. "I hear you said six months ago that I'm violent and that I'm a bully!"
The frightened lamb began to tremble and it replied quietly, "How can you believe such a thing? I have never said a bad word about you. Indeed, I will only be able to speak well of you in the future!" To its relief, the lamb remembered that it could prove its innocence, since it wasn't even born six months ago. "I wasn't here then, so I couldn't have spread any gossip about you."
But the wolf was only interested in gobbling up his prey, and so he quickly said, "Well, if it wasn't you, it was your father," and pouncing on the lamb, he quickly ate it.
Alas and alack! Innocence does not always save us from the clutches of a tyrant.

The Conceited Stag

Once upon a time . . . there was a stag who was very conceited. Every time he drank at a stream, he would stand and admire his reflection in the water. "I am so handsome," he would tell himself. "I have the finest set of antlers in the forest!"

Like all stags, he had long slender legs, but folk said he'd rather break a leg than lose a single branch of his antlers. Poor foolish stag! How vain he was.

One day, as he grazed peacefully on some tender shoots, he heard a distant shot and the barking of hounds . . . his enemies!

He knew that if the hounds caught his scent, it would not be easy to outrun them. He had to flee the hounds as quickly as possible.

As he sped through the forest, he could hear the barking of the pack at his heels.

Suddenly, his antlers got caught in the low-hanging branches of a tree. He shook his head vigorously, trying to break free, but his antlers were held fast.

The hounds were coming closer and closer. Just before the stag met his doom, he had time to think. "What a mistake I made! It is not my antlers that are the most precious part of my body, but my legs. They tried to carry me to safety, while my antlers will be the death of me!"

The Horse and the Wolf

Once upon a time . . . a horse was grazing peacefully in a rolling green meadow. A famished wolf passing by saw the horse and his mouth began to water.

"That's a fine horse! It will taste good too! It is a shame he is so big; I don't think I'll manage to bring him down, though one never knows —"
The wolf approached the horse; the horse continued to eat the grass. "Maybe if I take him by surprise . . . ," thought the wolf. From quite close, the wolf spoke to the horse, trying to sound as pleasant as he could. "Good day, Mr. Horse. I see you are enjoying a meal. Is the grass good? I must say you are looking rather pale. Are you well?"
His mouth full of grass, the horse replied, "Pale? Oh, no, it's my natural color. I was born white and gray." The wolf pretended not to understand. "Yes indeed, very pale. It is just as well your master has given you a holiday in the field, instead of working."
"A holiday?" said the horse. "But I am the picture of health!"
The wolf was circling the horse trying to find the best point of attack. "I am a doctor," said the wolf, "and I can treat you, if you tell me where the pain is. I can cure you! Take my advice and let me examine you!"
The horse was very suspicious of the wolf's remarks, and thought he had better be on guard. The wolf was very close by when the horse said, "Yes! Now that I think of it, I have a sore hind leg. It has been swollen for ages!" Without thinking, the wolf trotted up to the hoof that the horse had raised into the air.
When he was sure that the wolf was nearby, the horse gave a mighty kick and sent the wolf flying.
"Would you like to examine me again?" asked the horse, as the wolf was struggling to stand up, his head spinning.
"No, thank you, that is enough for one day," mumbled the wolf as he limped away. He was no longer hungry.

The Mouse and the Lion

Once upon a time . . . a little mouse, scampering over a lion he had chanced upon, happened to wake him up. The angry lion grabbed the mouse and held it to his jaws. “Don’t eat me, your Majesty,” the mouse pleaded, “If you let me go, I will never bother you again. I will always be grateful and will do you a good turn one day.” The lion had no intention of eating something so small; he had only wanted to frighten the mouse. “Well,” he chuckled, “a mouse that hopes to do a lion a good turn! Will you help me to hunt, or would you like to roar in my place?” The mouse did not know what to say. “Sire, I really . . . ,” he stammered.

“All right, you can go,” said the lion, opening his paw. The mouse scurried thankfully away.

Some days later, the lion fell into a trap and was caught in a net. Try as he might, he could not escape. The more he struggled, the more he became entangled in the mesh, until even his paws were held fast. He could not move an inch; it was the end. He could not use his strength, claws, or fangs to free himself. He was about to give up, when he heard a voice. “Do you need help?” asked the mouse. Exhausted, the lion looked around until he spotted the mouse.

“Oh, it’s you. I am afraid there is little you can do for me —”

The mouse interrupted him. “I can gnaw through the ropes. It will take me some time but I have strong teeth and I can manage.”

So the little mouse began to quickly chew on the ropes and soon the lion had one paw free, then another, and finally, he was free of the net.

“You see, Sire,” said the mouse, “I have done you a good turn in exchange for letting me go unharmed.”

“How right you are!” said the lion. “Never before has an animal so big been so grateful to an animal so very small!”

The Wolf and the Crane

Once upon a time . . . a wolf well-known for his ferocity received punishment for being greedy. As he was devouring a lamb, a small bone stuck in his throat and from that day on he could swallow nothing except sips of water. This neither soothed his pain nor appeased his hunger. He tried every remedy he knew, but he was unable to dislodge the bone. Desperate, he began to ask everyone he knew for help, but most were afraid of him and made excuses to avoid him.

One day he called on the fox, who refused to open the door, but he said, "I think you ought to have a word with the crane down at the big pond. They say she is the best doctor around."

Feeling hopeless, the wolf went to see the crane. When he got to her house, he tried his best to be pleasant. "Mrs. Crane, I am told that you are very clever. If you help me, I will give you a reward."

The crane was alarmed by the wolf's reputation, but at the same time, she was proud to have such a famous patient. Attracted by the reward, she promised to see what she could do.

The wolf opened his huge jaws. The crane shuddered at the thought of peering in among the sharp fangs, but gathering her courage, she said, "Now, keep your mouth wide open, or I will not be able to remove the bone." And she poked her long beak down the wolf's throat and pulled out the little bone. "There!" she said. "You can close your mouth now. You can now swallow whatever you like!" The wolf could hardly believe it — his throat was clear! Pleased, the crane said, "See how clever I am? And you didn't feel a thing. So about my reward —" Scowling, the wolf interrupted, "Reward? What reward?

You ought to be grateful that I did not bite your head off! You should give me a reward for sparing your life!" Looking into the wolf's eyes, the crane realized that she was in danger. What more could she expect from the wicked wolf? From then on, she vowed, she would only treat patients who were too harmless to ever threaten her.

The Horse and the Donkey

Once upon a time . . . an old carter kept a horse and a donkey in the same stable. He was equally fond of both of his animals, but since he used the horse to pull his trap, he gave it better food and more attention than he did the donkey.
The donkey, knowing he was not as precious as his stablemate, ate his straw without complaining.
When both animals carried sacks to market, the donkey's was the heavier load, for the carter did not want to overwork his noble horse. As time went by, the horse grew more handsome and robust, while the donkey became thin and weak.
One day, on their way to market, the donkey was carrying his usual heavy load, while the horse had only two lightweight sacks tied to the saddle. "I cannot go any further," moaned the donkey. "I am much weaker today. I will hardly be able to stand unless I get rid of some of this weight. Could you take some of my load?" he said to the horse.
The horse looked at the donkey in disdain and replied, "Our master gave you the heavy load because he knows that donkeys are beasts of burden. Their loads ought to be heavier than those of noble horses!"
The donkey stumbled on, but after a short while he said, "Please listen! If you do not help me, I will never reach the market alive." His tongue was hanging out, but the horse did not look at him and replied, "Nonsense! You'll manage this time, like you always do."
But after a few weak steps, the donkey dropped to the ground, dead. The donkey's master, who had fallen behind to pick

mushrooms, came running up. “Poor thing!” he said. “He served me well for so many years. His load must have been too heavy.” Then he turned to the horse. “Come here! You’ll have to carry his load now, too.” The master hoisted the donkey’s sacks onto the horse’s back. “I’d have done better to help the donkey when he was alive,” said the horse to himself. “A little more weight would have done me no harm. Now, I am afraid I will collapse under such a load!” But, feeling sorry too late did nothing to lighten the horse’s load.

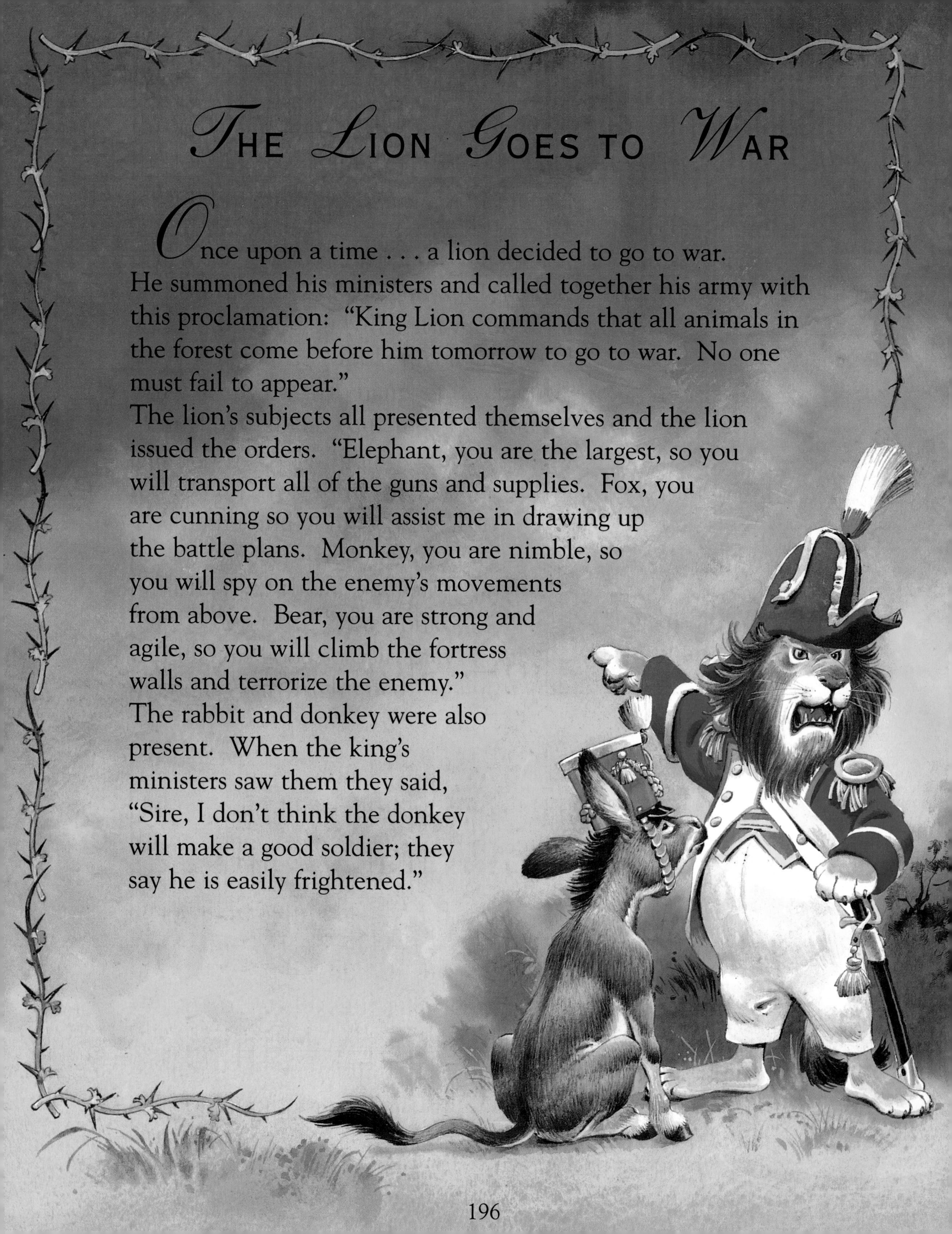

The Lion Goes to War

Once upon a time . . . a lion decided to go to war. He summoned his ministers and called together his army with this proclamation: "King Lion commands that all animals in the forest come before him tomorrow to go to war. No one must fail to appear."

The lion's subjects all presented themselves and the lion issued the orders. "Elephant, you are the largest, so you will transport all of the guns and supplies. Fox, you are cunning so you will assist me in drawing up the battle plans. Monkey, you are nimble, so you will spy on the enemy's movements from above. Bear, you are strong and agile, so you will climb the fortress walls and terrorize the enemy."

The rabbit and donkey were also present. When the king's ministers saw them they said, "Sire, I don't think the donkey will make a good soldier; they say he is easily frightened."

The lion looked at the donkey, and then he replied, “He can bray louder than I can roar. He will stay at my side and be the trumpet that will rally the troops.”

The king’s ministers then pointed to the rabbit. “He is even more nervous than the donkey; we should send him home.” The lion thought for a moment, and then he said to the rabbit, “You have learned that you must flee from your enemies to survive, so you will act as the messenger, and all of our soldiers will receive my orders within seconds.”

Turning to the crowd, the lion said, “Everyone can make himself or herself useful in a war, and everyone can help the common cause as best as he or she is able!”

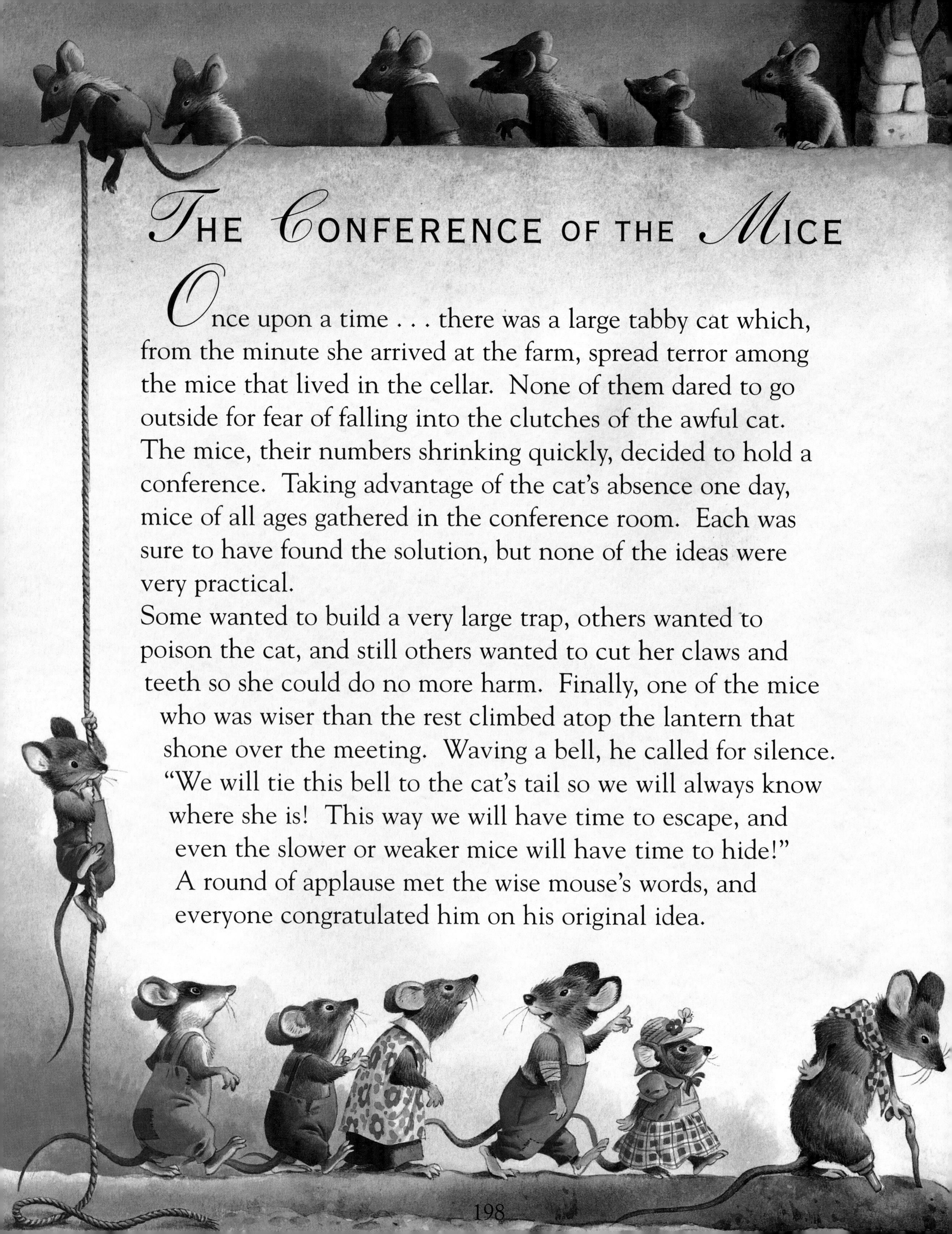

THE CONFERENCE OF THE MICE

Once upon a time . . . there was a large tabby cat which, from the minute she arrived at the farm, spread terror among the mice that lived in the cellar. None of them dared to go outside for fear of falling into the clutches of the awful cat. The mice, their numbers shrinking quickly, decided to hold a conference. Taking advantage of the cat's absence one day, mice of all ages gathered in the conference room. Each was sure to have found the solution, but none of the ideas were very practical.

Some wanted to build a very large trap, others wanted to poison the cat, and still others wanted to cut her claws and teeth so she could do no more harm. Finally, one of the mice who was wiser than the rest climbed atop the lantern that shone over the meeting. Waving a bell, he called for silence. "We will tie this bell to the cat's tail so we will always know where she is! This way we will have time to escape, and even the slower or weaker mice will have time to hide!"

A round of applause met the wise mouse's words, and everyone congratulated him on his original idea.

They all began discussing the benefits of the bell. However, the wise mouse again rang the bell for silence. “We must decide who is going to tie the bell onto the cat’s tail,” he said. There was silence. A few said quietly, “I can’t because —” or, “I’d do it willingly, but —” Not one of the mice was brave enough to come forward and put the plan into action. So, the conference of the mice ended without any decision being made. As the mice discovered, it is often very easy to have good ideas, but putting them into practice is a more difficult matter.

The Donkey that Thought he was Clever

Once upon a time . . . there was a donkey who thought he was very clever. Every day, his master harnessed him to a cart loaded with goods. They always went the same way to the village: through the woods, down a slope into the farmlands, along the river to the ford, and over the plain to the village. Since the route was always the same, the donkey's master often slept on top of the cart, while the donkey plodded on.
One day the man did not feel well, and he decided to send the donkey by himself, with a load that was to be delivered urgently. When the animal returned, he was given a double ration of oats as a reward.

"Since you are so clever," the man said, "I am going to send you alone, so I can do other jobs." From then on, in all kinds of weather, the donkey traveled to the village by himself.
His master was very pleased.
One morning, however, the donkey decided to shorten his journey by wading across the river. But he entered the river where it was deeper than he expected, and he had to swim. Luckily, he was carrying a load of salt that day, and some of it dissolved in the water, easing the donkey's load. He reached the other side without much difficulty. The donkey was pleased with himself; he had found a shortcut.
The next day, the man loaded the cart with sponges, and the donkey set off as usual. When he arrived at the river, he decided to take the shortcut and entered the water as before. But this time, the sponges soaked up the water and made the cart heavy, and the donkey could not keep his head above water. In spite of all of his efforts, the donkey that thought he was so clever sank below the surface together with his load.

The Monkey King

Once upon a time . . . a long time ago, there was a thick jungle where many kinds of animals lived together in harmony. Their ruler was a wise old lion. But one sad day, the king died and the animals had to decide who was to be their new ruler.

The king had a gold crown encrusted with precious gems, and it was decided that all of the candidates would come forward and try on the crown. The ruler would be the animal whose head it fitted best.

Many animals came forward and tried the crown on, but it fitted no one. Some heads were too big, or too small, others had horns or big ears. The fact was that the old king's crown did not fit any of the animals. Then a monkey snatched up the crown and began to amuse everyone with his clever tricks. He slipped it around his waist and twirled it like a hula-hoop. He tossed it high into the air and caught it as it came down. He stood on his head and twirled the crown on the tips of his toes, before jumping to his feet again and catching it in his hands.

The animals laughed and clapped at the nimble monkey's skill. Pleased, the monkey went on with his show until it was decided that the animals would give him the crown and proclaim him king. The only animal to disagree was the fox.

"We cannot have a silly creature like that as king!" he said. One day, the fox took a trap he had managed to avoid to the tree where the monkey lived. He covered it with dead leaves and picked a large bunch of bananas. He called up to the monkey, "Sire! I have some ripe bananas to present to you, but I cannot climb the tree as easily as you can. Would you come down and accept my gift?" The monkey climbed down the tree and just as he reached for the bananas, the trap closed over his legs. The fox laughed. "What a foolish king we have!" He called to the other animals. "Just look at our sovereign! He can't even avoid being caught in a trap, and all for a handful of bananas! If he cannot watch out for himself, how can he watch out for us?" The animals let themselves be persuaded by the fox's words, and soon enough, the monkey had his crown taken away. From that day on, this particular jungle was the only one whose animals did not have a king.

A Fairy Tale by CARLO COLLODI

The Author of "Pinocchio" - Carlo Collodi's real name was actually Carlo Lorenzini. He was born on November 24, 1826 in Florence, Italy, and died in the same city on October 26, 1890. Collodi is famous all over the world for having written the story of "Pinocchio." He began writing stories for children in 1861, and wrote the adventure of "Pinocchio" in 1881. The first chapter appeared in a children's magazine called *Il giornale dei bambini*, and quickly became very popular. "Pinocchio" was published as a book in 1883.

The Wooden Puppet - Pinocchio, the main character of the story, is a puppet made of wood, but he looks very much like a normal little boy. He wants to do good and to please his father, but he is often very bad, and when he tells a lie, his nose grows, and grows, and grows.

Puppet theatre was a popular form of entertainment for children and adults in the 1800s; these puppets were often made out of wood.

Right, a typical view of the hills of Florence in Collodi's day.

There Was Much to Do . . . in Italy during the movement for national unification, and Carlo Lorenzini worked as a journalist, helping his country in the fight against Austrian rule. In 1861, the Kingdom of Italy was formed, and Collodi turned to writing for children.

Be Good! . . . This is what Pinocchio tried to do, yet he rarely succeeded. Still, his father always forgave him. Perhaps it was Gepetto's unending faith that gave Pinocchio the courage to be good: the story shows that even naughty little children can behave very well, in the end.

Geppetto is by trade a cobbler, that is, someone who repairs or makes shoes. (Once upon a time, many shoes had wooden heels or soles.) He makes Pinocchio out of a piece of wood that is given to him by a friend. But it is no ordinary piece of wood! As soon as Pinocchio's features are formed, he begins to move just like a human being. However, he is very naughty!

PINOCCHIO

Once upon a time . . . a carpenter picked up a strange lump of wood while mending a table. When he began to whittle it, the wood started to moan. The frightened carpenter decided to get rid of it at once. He gave it to his friend, the cobbler Geppetto, who wanted to make a puppet.

"I'll call him Pinocchio," mused the cobbler. "That's a lucky name."

Back in his workshop, Geppetto started to carve the wood.

Suddenly a voice squealed, "Ooh! That hurt!"

Geppetto was astonished. Excitement mounting, he carved a head, then eyes that immediately stared right at the cobbler. But the moment Geppetto carved the nose, it grew longer and longer, no matter how often the cobbler cut it down to size.

The newly carved mouth began to chuckle.

"Be still!" scolded Geppetto, but the puppet rudely stuck out his tongue. By the time the cobbler had shaped the hands and feet, the wooden puppet was ready to snatch off the good man's wig and give him a hearty kick.

"You naughty boy!" murmured Geppetto reproachfully.

"I haven't even finished making you, yet you have no respect for me — your own father!"

Nevertheless, the kind old fellow picked up the puppet, and, one step at a time, taught him to walk. But the minute Pinocchio could manage his legs he ran wildly about the room, then out the door and into the street.
"Stop him!" shouted the cobbler. The passersby just laughed. Luckily, a policeman heard the cobbler's shouts and quickly grabbed the runaway, handing him over to his father.
"I'm sorry, Father," said Pinocchio.
Geppetto forgave his son and made him a jacket of flowered paper, a pair of plain trousers, some bark shoes, and a bread hat.
"How smart I look!" said Pinocchio, hugging his father. "I'd like to go to school so I can help you when you're old."
"What a thoughtful boy," said Geppetto. "But we haven't enough money even to buy a first reader." Pinocchio's mouth drooped.
Geppetto suddenly rose, put on his old coat, and left the house. Soon he returned, carrying a first reader, but not wearing his coat. It was snowing outside. "Where's your coat, Father?"

"I sold it because it kept me too warm," Geppetto replied.
Pinocchio threw his arms around Geppetto's neck and kissed him.
The next day it had stopped snowing, and Pinocchio set out for school with his reader tucked under his arm, full of good intentions. "Today I'll learn to read, tomorrow to write, and the next day I'll learn to count," he said to himself. "Then I'll earn the money for a new coat for Geppetto —" But alas, the sound of a brass band broke into the puppet's daydream, and he forgot all about school.
In the town square, people were clustering around a brightly-colored booth. "What's that?" Pinocchio asked a bystander. "Read the sign! It says, 'Great Puppet Show: Four Pennies a Person'."
"Who'll give me four pennies for this brand new book?" Pinocchio cried. A junk dealer quickly bought the reader, and Pinocchio hurried into the booth. Poor Geppetto, his sacrifice had been quite in vain! Hardly had Pinocchio got inside than the puppets on stage began to shout, "Pinocchio! Come and join us. Hurrah for brother Pinocchio!" The giddy boy rushed onto the stage and chattered with his new friends. The spectators began to mutter.

Out strode the puppet master, Fire-Eater, a hulking man with a long black beard and bushy eyebrows that made him look very fierce. "What's going on here!" he roared. "Stop that noise!"
That evening, when Fire-Eater sat down to dinner, he found his mutton half-cooked. "Humph! The stove needs more wood," he thought, then he remembered the intruder who had upset his show. "Come here, Pinocchio. At least you're good for something!" he shouted. The puppet burst into tears. "Save me, Father! I don't want to die!" Fire-Eater was taken aback. "You have parents?" he asked. "A father — but I never knew a mother," said the puppet in a low voice. The big man's heart melted. "Well, I'll take pity on your father," he said, "but I must finish roasting the mutton. Bring me Harlequin!" When Pinocchio saw that another puppet would be burned instead, he cried harder than ever. "Oh, please don't burn Harlequin!"
"Enough!" boomed Fire-Eater. "I want my meat properly cooked."
"In that case, burn me," said Pinocchio defiantly.
Fire-Eater was dumbfounded. "Well! I've never met a puppet hero before!" At last the man said, "All right, but next time somebody is going to find himself in a pickle!"
The puppeteer asked about Pinocchio's father and the puppet told him the whole story. "Here, take these to him," he said, handing the boy five gold pieces, "and tell him to buy a new coat."
Pinocchio thanked Fire-Eater and cheerfully left the puppet booth.

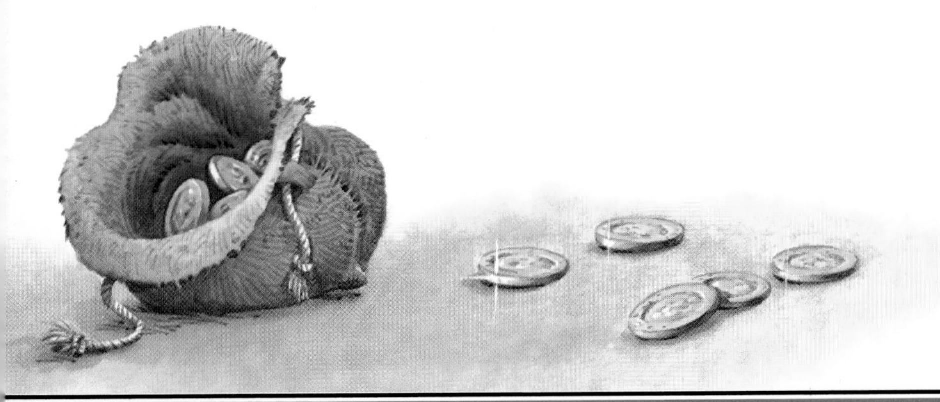

He was hurrying homeward when he met with a half-blind cat and a lame fox. He couldn't help telling them all about his good fortune.
The pair peered greedily at the gold coins. "If you'd really like to please your father," said the crafty fox, "we know of a meadow where you can sow these five coins. The next day, you'll find ten times as many!"

The gullible puppet followed the fox and the cat, who led him to the edge of a meadow. "See that big, dead tree?" said the fox. "Dig a hole at the foot of it, and bury your gold. We'll wait here."

Night was falling when Pinocchio set off. Before he had gone very far, two shapes loomed up.
"Your money or your life!" growled one in a suspiciously fox-like voice. The puppet had hidden the gold coins under his tongue and couldn't speak. He stared in silent fear.
"Well!" said the robbers, hanging Pinocchio from the tree, "You'll hang there until you decide to talk. We'll be back soon." The wicked pair then snuck away.
Pinocchio didn't know what to do. As luck would have it, a fairy passed by. "What happened?" she asked, clapping her hands for her pet woodpeckers. The birds pecked the rope to pieces. Thump! Pinocchio sat down hard and nearly swallowed the coins. He slipped them in his pocket for safekeeping.
After his misadventure, Pinocchio fell quite ill, but the kind fairy took care of him.

She called three famous doctors to cure him: the wise owl, the crow, and the cricket.

When Pinocchio finally got better, the fairy asked him what had happened. Pinocchio told his story, but left out the part about selling the reader. His nose began to grow longer and longer.

"Goodness, you must be fibbing!" laughed the fairy. "I can tell because your nose is growing." She clapped her hands again, and

the woodpeckers came and pecked Pinocchio's nose down to size.
"Go straight home to your father, now," scolded the fairy.
But foolish Pinocchio went to the meadow, instead, and
buried the coins at the foot of the dead tree.
He waited under a bush until dawn, then hurried back, only
to find an empty hole!
Pinocchio trudged sadly home. Geppetto was overjoyed
and again forgave his son's thoughtlessness.
Pinocchio set off for school once more, full of good intentions.
Alas, there he met Wick, the laziest boy in the class.

"Why don't you come to Toyland with me?" said Wick. "Nobody ever studies there, and you can play all day long!"
"Does such a place really exist?" asked Pinocchio in amazement.
"The wagon is coming by this evening to take me there. Would you like to come?" Forgetting all his good intentions, Pinocchio joined his new-found friend.
Midnight struck and the wagon arrived, filled with boisterous schoolboys. Twelve pairs of sad little donkeys wearing boots pulled the wagon.
Pinocchio was too excited to notice any of this, and clambered up on the back of a donkey. "Hurrah! We're off!" he shouted.
Toyland was just as Wick had said it would be. No one was even allowed to whisper the word "school."

"This is the life!" Pinocchio exclaimed whenever he met Wick.
"I was right, wasn't I?" said his friend smugly.
One day, however, Pinocchio awoke to a nasty surprise. When he raised a hand to his head, he found he had sprouted a long pair of hairy ears! By the next day, they were longer than ever.
Pinocchio pulled on a large cotton cap to hide his ears and went off in search of his friend.
Wick too was wearing a hat pulled right down to his nose. The two boys stared at each other, then snatched off their hats, roaring with laughter at the funny sight.
But as they laughed, Wick suddenly went pale and began to stagger. "Pinocchio, help!" he cried, but Pinocchio himself was stumbling about, and he burst into tears as he felt himself go down on all fours. Pinocchio and Wick were turning into donkeys!

They tried to cry out, but they brayed loudly instead.
When the Toyland wagon driver heard the braying of his new donkeys, he rubbed his hands with glee.
"Two fine new donkeys for market. I'll get at least four gold pieces for them!" Such was the fate of boys who played hooky!
The wagon driver sold Wick to a farmer, and Pinocchio to a circus man, who taught him to do tricks like his other performing animals.
One day, however, as he was jumping through the hoop, Pinocchio stumbled and went lame.
The circus man took Pinocchio to market and tried to sell him, but nobody wanted to buy a lame donkey. Then a leather-maker came along, who bought Pinocchio for a few pennies.

The tanner led the donkey to a cliff and tied a rope around its hind leg. As the poor animal looked at the waves, the man kicked it right over the edge!
Pinocchio struggled with all his might, thinking of his father.
Suddenly a school of little fish appeared and began to nibble away at the donkey skin.

Just as they had finished,
Pinocchio felt himself being
hauled up by the leg.
"Where's my donkey skin?" gasped
the tanner, reaching for Pinocchio.
"That was me!" giggled Pinocchio
nervously, nimbly slipping his foot
out of the rope.

"Twenty coins for a stick!" shouted the
tanner angrily. "I'll sell you for firewood."
"Oh, no you won't," said Pinocchio.
With a twist and a leap he dodged the
tanner and dove head first into the sea.
It so happened that, at this very moment,
a huge whale came gliding by, jaws wide
open to catch anything in its path.

"Help!" cried Pinocchio, swimming as hard as he could. But a wave washed him into the cavernous mouth and down he went, tossed in the strong torrent of water that poured down the whale's throat.
When Pinocchio came to his senses, everything was pitch black. Overhead he could hear the loud heave of the whale's gills.
The puppet crept on all fours along what seemed like a sloping path, crying as he went, "Help! Won't anybody save me?"
Suddenly a flickering light appeared ahead.
And what was that? A battered table and chair? A candle stuck in a bottle? And a man —
"Father! Is it really you!"
"Pinocchio! Son!"

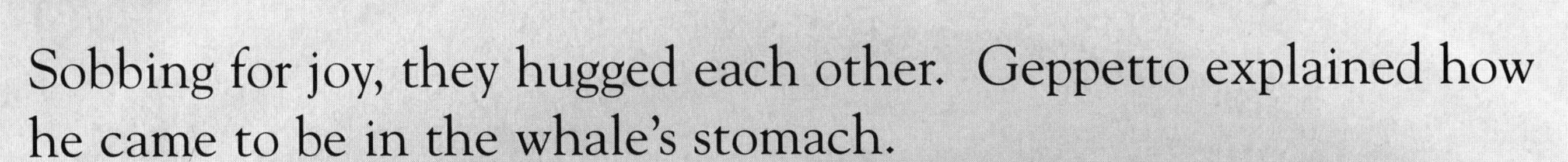

Sobbing for joy, they hugged each other. Geppetto explained how he came to be in the whale's stomach.

"When I couldn't find you on land, I made a boat to search for you on the sea. But the boat sank in a storm, and the whale gulped me down. Luckily, it also swallowed bits of shipwreck, so I have managed to survive."

"We must get out of here!" urged Pinocchio, taking Geppetto's hand.
"I think the whale should be asleep now," said Geppetto.

The pair started to climb up the whale's stomach, using a candle to light the way. They crept along the whale's tongue and right up to the edge of its mouth. "Now is our chance to escape," whispered Pinocchio. In a second he was in the water, swimming as quickly as he could, with Geppetto on his back.

Luckily, the whale had been basking in shallow waters since the day before, and they soon reached the shore. On the beach was an old hut, and they took shelter. Geppetto was weak from hunger.
"I'm going to get you some milk," said Pinocchio.
He walked until he reached a nearby farm, but he had no money to pay for the milk. "If you work the treadmill, you can have some milk," said the farmer. And so, for days, Pinocchio rose early each morning to earn Geppetto's food. At last, Geppetto was well and he and Pinocchio could return home.
The puppet worked late into the night weaving baskets to make money for his father and himself. One night, in a dream, the fairy appeared to reward Pinocchio for his kindness. The next morning, Pinocchio rose as usual. But when he looked in the mirror . . . he saw a real boy with blue eyes, real hair, and . . . a small nose!
Geppetto gasped when he saw his son. He hugged him.
"What happened to my old wooden self?" wondered Pinocchio.
"There!" exclaimed Geppetto, pointing to a shape slumped on a chair. "I couldn't carve a heart for the old Pinocchio, but because of your hard work and kindness, you made one for yourself!"

Fairy Tales of CHARLES PERRAULT

Tales of Mother Goose **-** This was the title of Charles Perrault's famous collection of children's fairy tales. It was written in 1697. He wrote this collection of stories for his own children, to keep them entertained. Since Perrault believed in the evolution of language, he rewrote famous oral fairy tales but in a modern style, making them very popular in France, and around the world.

Charles Perrault was born on January 12, 1628 in Paris, France, and died on May 15, 1703. He was a poet who supported literature and the arts.

The Ancients and the Moderns - In the 1670s in France there was a great literary debate. The moderns, like Perrault, believed that as civilization moved forward, language developed and grew as well; therefore modern language was best.

Various Academies . . . were created in Europe, beginning in the 16th century. They were especially numerous in Italy. Academies were founded to promote national languages and literatures. Charles Perrault was elected to the Académie Française in 1671. Other French writers, such as Jean de la Fontaine, were also members of the Académie Française.

Above, an inkwell with candles for illumination, and a mirror. This was a typical decorative object found in France in the late 1600s.
Behind the inkwell is a collection of gazettes, French newspapers of the time.

Before Perrault . . . there were some other collections of fairy tales existing in Europe, such as *The Story of Stories* written by G. Basile in Italy in 1634. "Puss in Boots" and "Cinderella" were found in this Italian collection.

Other famous stories that Perrault has retold include "Little Red Riding Hood" and "Bluebeard."

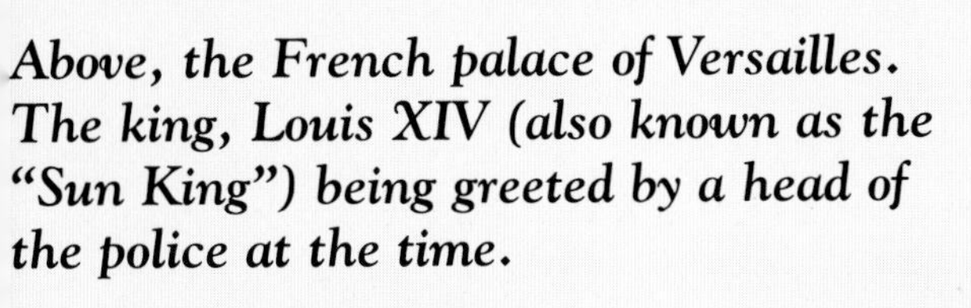

Above, the French palace of Versailles. The king, Louis XIV (also known as the "Sun King") being greeted by a head of the police at the time.

At right, "Cinderella" is the story of a young girl who goes to a ball and meets a prince — but she must return home by midnight or her carriage will turn into a pumpkin!

Little Red Riding Hood

Once upon a time . . . in the middle of a thick forest stood a small cottage, the home of a pretty little girl known to everyone as Little Red Riding Hood. One day, her mother waved her goodbye at the garden gate, saying, "Grandma is ill. Take her this basket of cakes, but be very careful. Keep to the path through the woods and don't stop. That way, you will come to no harm."
"Don't worry," said Little Red Riding Hood, "I'll run all the way to Grandma's without stopping."

The little girl made her way through the woods, but she was soon to forget her mother's words.
"What lovely strawberries! And so red . . . ," she thought.
Laying her basket on the ground, Little Red Riding Hood bent over the strawberry plants. "They're nice and ripe, and so big! Yummy!" Little Red Riding Hood ran back and forth popping strawberries into her mouth. Suddenly she remembered Grandma . . . and hurried back towards the path. She picked up her basket and, humming to herself, Little Red Riding Hood walked on.

The woods became thicker and thicker. Suddenly she saw some large daisies in the grass.
"Oh, how sweet!" she exclaimed and, thinking of Grandma, she picked a large bunch of flowers.
In the meantime, two wicked eyes were spying on her from behind a tree . . . a strange rustling in the woods made her heart thump.

Suddenly, she heard the sound of a gruff voice: "Where are you going, my pretty girl, all alone in the woods?"
"I'm taking Grandma some cakes," said Little Red Riding Hood, in a trembling voice.
The big bad wolf asked, "Does Grandma live all by herself?"
"Oh, yes," replied Little Red Riding Hood, "and she never opens the door to strangers!"

“Goodbye. Perhaps we’ll meet again,” replied the wolf.
Then he loped away thinking to himself, “I’ll gobble the grandmother first, then lie in wait for the grandchild!”
At last, the cottage came into sight. The wolf rapped on the door.
“Who’s there?” cried Grandma from her bed.
“It’s me, Little Red Riding Hood. I’ve brought you some cakes,” replied the wolf, trying to hide his gruff voice.
“Come in,” said Grandma. A horrible shadow appeared on the wall. Poor Grandma! In one bound, the wolf leapt across the room and, in a single mouthful, swallowed the old lady.

Soon after, Little Red Riding Hood tapped on the door.
"Grandma, can I come in?" she called.
Now, the wolf had put on the old lady's shawl and cap and slipped into bed. Trying to imitate Grandma's quavering voice, he replied, "Open the latch and come in!"
"What a deep voice you have," said the little girl in surprise.
"The better to greet you with," said the wolf.
"Goodness, what big eyes you have," she replied.
"The better to see you with," explained the wolf.
"And what big hands you have!" exclaimed Little Red Riding Hood.
"The better to hug you with," said the wolf.
"What a big mouth you have," the little girl murmured.
"The better to eat you with!" growled the wolf, and jumping out of bed, he swallowed her up. Then, with a full tummy, he fell asleep.

In the meantime, a hunter passing by the cottage, decided to stop and ask for a drink. He had been trying to catch a large wolf, but had lost its tracks. The hunter could hear a strange whistling sound coming from inside the cottage. He peered through the window . . . and saw the large wolf, with a fat tummy, snoring away in Grandma's bed.
"The wolf! He won't get away this time!" he thought. Silently, the hunter loaded his gun and opened the window. He pointed the barrel straight at the wolf's head and . . . BANG! The wolf was dead.
"Got you at last!" shouted the hunter, "and you'll never frighten anyone again."
He cut open the wolf's stomach and to his amazement,

out popped Grandma and Little Red Riding Hood, safe and unharmed. "You arrived just in time," said the old lady.

"It's safe to go home now," the hunter told Little Red Riding Hood. "The big bad wolf is dead, and there is no danger on the path."

Much later, Little Red Riding Hood's mother arrived, worried because her little girl had not come home. When she saw Little Red Riding Hood, safe and sound, she burst into tears of joy.

After thanking the hunter again, Little Red Riding Hood and her mother set off towards home. As they walked quickly through the woods, the little girl told her mother, "We must always keep to the path and never stop. That way, we'll come to no harm."

Puss in Boots

Once upon a time . . . a miller died leaving the mill to his eldest son, his donkey to his second son, and a cat to his youngest son. The eldest son kept the mill, the second son took the donkey and

set off in search of his fortune, while the third sat down on a stone and sighed.
"A cat! What am I going to do with that?" But the cat heard his words and said, "Don't worry, Master. What do you think? That I'm worth less than a half-ruined mill or an old donkey? Give me a cloak, a hat with a feather in it, a bag, and a pair of boots, and you'll see what I can do."
The young man gave the cat what he asked for, and as he strode away, the cat said, "Don't look so glum, Master. I'll see you soon."
By and by, the cat caught a fat wild rabbit, popped it into his bag, knocked at the castle gate, and went before the King.

Removing his hat, with a sweeping bow, he said,
"Sire, the famous Marquis of Carabas sends you this fine plump rabbit as a gift."
"Oh," said the King, "Thank you very much indeed!"

The next day, the cat came back with some partridges.
"Another gift from the brave Marquis of Carabas," he announced.
In the days that followed, Puss in Boots regularly visited the castle, carrying rabbits, hares, partridges, and skylarks, presenting them all to the King in the name of the Marquis of Carabas. Folk at the palace began to talk about this noble gentleman.
"He must be a great hunter," someone remarked. "He must be very loyal to the King," said someone else. And yet another,
"But who is he? I've never heard of him."
"Is your master young and handsome?" the Queen asked the cat.
"Oh, yes, and very rich, too," answered Puss in Boots.
"In fact, he would be very honored if you and the King called to see him in his castle."
The cat returned home and told his master that the King and Queen were going to visit him.
"Whatever shall we do?" he cried. "As soon as they see me they will know how poor I am."
"Leave everything to me," replied Puss in Boots. "I have a plan."
For several days, the crafty cat kept on taking gifts to the King and Queen. One day he discovered that they were taking the Princess on a carriage ride that very afternoon.

The cat hurried home in great excitement. “Master, come along,” he cried. “It is time to carry out my plan. You must go for a swim in the river.”

“But I can’t swim,” replied the young man.

“That’s all right,” replied Puss in Boots. “Just trust me.”

So they went to the river and when the King’s carriage appeared, the cat pushed his master into the water.

“Help!” cried the cat. “The Marquis of Carabas is drowning.”

The King heard his cry and sent his escorts to the rescue. They arrived just in time to save the poor man. The King, the Queen, and the Princess fussed over the Marquis of Carabas.

“Wouldn’t you like to marry such a handsome man?” the Queen asked her daughter.

“Oh, yes,” replied the Princess. However, the cat overheard the King remark that they must find out how rich he was.

“He is very rich indeed,” said Puss in Boots. “He owns the castle and all this land. Come and see for yourself. I will meet you at the castle.”

The cat rushed off toward the castle, shouting at the peasants working in the fields, “If anyone asks you who your master is, say: the Marquis of Carabas.” So, when the King’s carriage passed by,

the peasants told the King that their master was the Marquis of Carabas.

Puss in Boots arrived at the castle, the home of a huge, mean ogre. Before knocking at the gate, the cat said to himself, "I must be very careful, or I'll never get out alive."

When the door opened, Puss in Boots removed his feather hat, exclaiming, "My Lord Ogre, my respects!"
"What do you want, cat?" asked the ogre.
"Sire, I've heard you possess great powers. That, for instance, you can change into a lion or an elephant."
"That's perfectly true," said the ogre, "and so what?"
"Well," said the cat, "I bet you can't turn into a tiny little creature, like a mouse."
"Oh, yes? Well, just watch this!" said the ogre, turning into a mouse. In a flash, the cat leapt on the mouse and ate it whole. Then he dashed to the castle gate, just as the King's carriage was drawing up.
With a bow, Puss in Boots said, "Sire, welcome to the castle of the Marquis of Carabas!" The King and Queen, the Princess, and the miller's son got out of the carriage.
The King spoke:
"My dear Marquis, you're a fine, handsome, young man. You have a great deal of land and a magnificent castle. Tell me, are you married?"
"No," the young man answered, "but I would like to find a wife." He looked at the Princess as he spoke.
She in turn smiled.
To make a long story short, the miller's son married the Princess and lived happily with her in the castle.
And from time to time, the cat would wink and whisper, "You see, Master, I am worth a lot more than any old donkey or half-ruined mill, aren't I?"

CINDERELLA

Once upon a time . . . there was a beautiful, sweet young girl who was very unhappy. Her mother had died and her father had married another woman. Unfortunately, her stepmother and her two stepsisters did not like her one bit. While her stepsisters had all the comforts of life, the poor girl was treated like a servant. She had to work hard all day, and only when evening came was she allowed to sit for a while by the fire, near the cinders. That is how she got her

nickname, Cinderella. Cinderella used to spend long hours all alone talking to the cat. The cat would say, "Meow," which really meant, "Cheer up! You have something neither of your stepsisters have: beauty." It was quite true. Cinderella, even dressed in rags and with a dusty gray face from the cinders, was a lovely girl. While her stepsisters, no matter how splendid and elegant their clothes, were clumsy, and ugly. One day, beautiful new dresses were delivered to the house. A ball was to be held at Court and the stepsisters were getting ready to go to it. Cinderella didn't dare ask,

"What about me?" for she knew very well what the answer would be.
"You're staying at home to wash the dishes and scrub the floors."
"Oh dear, I'm so unhappy!" Cinderella sighed to the cat.
Suddenly something amazing happened. There was a burst of light and a fairy appeared!
"Don't be alarmed, Cinderella," said the fairy. "The wind blew me your sighs. I know you would love to go to the ball. And you shall!"
"How can I, dressed in rags?" Cinderella replied.
The fairy smiled. With a flick of her magic wand . . .

. . . Cinderella found herself wearing a beautiful ball gown.
"Now," said the fairy, "We'll need to get you a coach. A real lady would never go to a ball on foot! Quick! Get me a pumpkin!" she ordered. "Oh, of course," said Cinderella, rushing away.
Then the fairy turned to the cat, "You, bring me seven mice!"
Cinderella soon returned with a fine pumpkin and the cat with seven mice. "Good!" exclaimed the fairy. With a flick of her magic wand, the pumpkin turned into a sparkling coach and the mice became six white horses, while the seventh mouse turned into a coachman.
Cinderella could hardly believe her eyes.
"You are now ready to go to the ball. The Prince will be enchanted by your loveliness. But remember! You must leave at midnight. That is when the spell ends. Your coach will turn back into a pumpkin and the horses and coachman will become mice again . . . and you will be dressed once again in rags and wearing clogs instead of these dainty slippers! Do you understand?"
Cinderella smiled and said, "Yes, I understand!"

When Cinderella entered the ballroom at the palace, a hush fell. Everyone stopped to admire her elegance, beauty, and grace. "Who can that be?" people asked each other. Even the two stepsisters would never have guessed that the beautiful girl was really poor Cinderella.

When the Prince set eyes on Cinderella, he walked over to her, bowed deeply, and asked her to dance. In fact, he danced with Cinderella all evening.

"Who are you, fair maiden?" the Prince kept asking her.

But Cinderella only replied, "What does it matter who I am? You will never see me again anyway."

"Oh, but I shall, I'm quite certain!" he replied.

Cinderella was having a wonderful time at the ball . . .

. . . when all of a sudden, she heard the first stroke of midnight!
Remembering what the fairy had said, Cinderella quickly said goodbye to the Prince. As she ran down the stairs she lost one of her slippers! But she had no time to stop and pick it up. If the last stroke of midnight were to sound . . . what a disaster that would be! She fled from the palace and vanished into the night.

The Prince, who was now madly in love with her, picked up her slipper and said to his ministers, “Go and search everywhere for the girl whose foot fits this slipper. I will not be content until I find her!” So the ministers tried the slipper on the foot of all the girls in the kingdom, but it didn’t fit any of them.
Finally, they came to Cinderella’s house. The two stepsisters struggled in vain to fit their big feet into the little slipper.

Then one of the ministers noticed Cinderella and asked her to try it on. The slipper fit perfectly!
At that very moment, the fairy appeared and raised her magic wand. In a flash, Cinderella's rags were transformed into a splendid dress. Her stepmother and stepsisters gaped at her in amazement, and the ministers said, "Come with us, fair maiden! The Prince awaits to present you with an engagement ring!" So Cinderella joyfully went with them to the palace, and lived happily ever after with her Prince.
And as for the cat, he just said, "Meow!"

Beauty and the Beast

Once upon a time . . . as a merchant set off for market, he asked each of his three daughters what she would like as a present on his return. The first daughter wanted a brocade dress, the second a pearl necklace, but the third, whose name was Beauty, the youngest, prettiest, and sweetest of them all, said to her father, "All I'd like is a rose you've picked especially for me!"

When the merchant had finished his business, he set off for home. However, a sudden storm blew up. Cold and tired, the merchant lost all hope of reaching an inn. Suddenly, he noticed a light shining in the middle of a wood. As he drew near, he saw that it was a castle. When he reached the door, he saw it was open, and though he shouted, nobody came to greet him. He went inside. On a table in the main hall, a splendid dinner lay already served. No one answered his calls, so the hungry merchant sat down to a warm meal. Curious, he went upstairs, where the hall led into magnificent rooms. A fire crackled in the first room and a soft bed looked very inviting. It was now late. He lay down on the bed and fell fast asleep.

When he woke the next morning, he found a mug of steaming coffee and some fruit by his bedside.

The merchant had breakfast and went downstairs to thank his host. But there was no one in sight. He wandered outside and then into the garden. Suddenly, a large rose bush caught his eye.

Remembering his promise to Beauty, he bent down to pick a rose especially for her. Instantly, out sprang a horrible beast wearing

splendid clothes. A deep, terrifying voice growled, "Ungrateful man! I gave you shelter, you ate at my table and slept in my own bed, but now all the thanks I get is the theft of my favorite flowers! I shall put you to death!"

Trembling with fear, the merchant fell on his knees before the beast. "Forgive me! I'll do anything you say! The rose was for my daughter, Beauty. I promised to bring her back a rose!"

"I shall spare your life, but on one condition, that you bring me your daughter!" The terror-stricken merchant promised that he would. He arrived home in tears and told his daughters his dreadful adventure. Beauty put his mind at rest immediately.
"Dear father, don't worry. Take me to the castle. I'll stay there in your place!" The merchant hugged his daughter.
"I never did doubt your love for me. Thank you for saving my life."
So Beauty was led to the castle. Surprisingly, the Beast greeted the girl pleasantly.
At first, Beauty was frightened of the Beast. Then she found that, in spite of the monster's awful head, her horror of it gradually faded as time went by. She had one of the finest rooms in the castle and sat for hours, embroidering in front of the fire. And the Beast would sit, only a short distance away, silently gazing at her.

Then it started to say a few kind words, till in the end, Beauty was actually enjoying its company.
The days passed, and Beauty and the Beast became good friends. Then one day, the Beast asked the girl to be his wife.
Taken by surprise, Beauty did not know what to say. Marry such an ugly monster? She would rather die! But she did not want to hurt its feelings. She owed to it her own life as well as her father's.
"I really can't say yes. I'd so much like to —"
The Beast interrupted her. "I quite understand! And I'm not offended by your refusal!" Life went on as usual, and nothing further was said. One day, the Beast presented Beauty with a magic mirror. When Beauty peered into it, she could see her family, far away.
"You won't feel so lonely now," said the Beast. Beauty stared for hours at her distant family.

One day, the Beast found her weeping beside the magic mirror.
"What's wrong?" he asked, kindly as always.
"My father is very ill and close to dying! Oh, how I wish I could see him again, before it's too late!"
"If you swear that you will return here in seven days' time, I'll let you go and visit your father!"
"I swear! I swear I will! How kind you are! You've made a loving daughter so happy!" replied Beauty.
Beauty returned to her father and stayed beside him for hours, describing her life at the castle, and explaining that the Beast was really good and kind. The days passed and at last the merchant was able to leave his bed. He was completely well again. Beauty was happy. However, she had not noticed that seven days had gone by. Then one night she woke from a terrible nightmare. She had dreamt that the Beast was dying and calling for her.
"Come back! Come back to me!" it was pleading. Beauty remembered her promise and left home immediately.

Once at the castle, she ran into the garden and there crouched the Beast, its eyes shut as though dead. Beauty threw herself at it and hugged it tightly.
"Don't die! Don't die! I'll marry you —" At these words, the Beast magically turned into a handsome young man.
"How I've been longing for this moment!" he said. "An evil witch turned me into a monster, and only the love of a maiden willing to accept me as I was could change me back into my real self. My dearest! I'll be so happy if you'll marry me!"
Soon the wedding took place and, from that day on, the young prince would have nothing but roses in his gardens. And that's why, to this day, the castle is known as the Castle of the Rose.

Bluebeard

Once upon a time . . . there lived a very rich and powerful lord whose name was Bluebeard. He was given this nickname because he had a long, shaggy black beard with glints of blue in it. He was very handsome, but there was something about him that made people feel a little uneasy —

Bluebeard had had lots of wives, all young, pretty, and noble.
But, one after the other, they had all died, and so the noble lord was forever getting married again.
"Sire," someone would ask, "what did your wives die of?"
"Hah, my friend," Bluebeard would reply, "I'm very unlucky, and they're unlucky too!"
Soon Bluebeard got married again and he brought his sweet and beautiful young bride to his castle. The young girl's sister, Anna, came along too, to keep her company.
"Aren't you lucky marrying a lord like Bluebeard!" remarked Anna.
"He really is very nice . . . and from up close, his beard doesn't look as blue as they say!" replied the bride. But, the two girls had no idea what lay in store for them!

A month later, Bluebeard said to his wife, "Darling, I must leave you for a few weeks. Look after the castle. Here," he added, handing his bride a bunch of keys, "you'll need these to open the doors of the different rooms. This little key here," and he pointed to a key much smaller than the others, "opens the little room at the end of the corridor. Open any door you like, but not that one! Is that clear?" stressed Bluebeard. "Nobody at all is allowed to enter that room."
"Don't worry," said Bluebeard's wife. "I'll do as you say."
After giving her a hug, Bluebeard got into his carriage and rode off.
The days went by. The young girl invited her friends to the castle and showed them around, except the room at the end of the corridor.
"Why shouldn't I see inside the little room?" she wondered.
She thought about it so much that one day she opened the door and walked in . . . Horrors! Inside the room, hanging on the walls, were the bodies of Bluebeard's previous wives!

Terror stricken, the girl ran out of the room, but the bunch of keys slipped from her grasp. She picked it up and hurried to her own room, her heart thumping wildly. She was living in a castle of the dead! So that is what had happened to Bluebeard's other wives! The girl noticed that the key to the room was stained with blood. "I must wipe it clean, before my husband comes back!" she said to herself. But try as she would, the blood stain wouldn't wash away. That very evening, Bluebeard came home.

Just imagine the state his poor wife was in! "You look a little upset, darling. Has anything nasty happened?" he asked. "Oh, no! I'm delighted you're back!" she replied. But that night, the bride didn't sleep a wink. The next day, Bluebeard said, "Darling, give me back the keys," and his wife hurriedly did so. Bluebeard said, "There's one missing, the key to the little room!"

"I must have left it in my room!" said the young girl, shaking.
"All right, go and get it," he replied. But when Bluebeard's wife put the key into his hand, Bluebeard shouted angrily,
"Why is this key stained with blood?"
"I don't know . . . ," stammered his wife.
"You know very well!" he yelled. "You went into the little room, didn't you? Well, you'll go back again, for good — you must die!"
"Oh, no! I pray you!" cried his wife.
Just then, there was a knock at the door and Anna, Bluebeard's wife's sister, came in.
Bluebeard's wife whispered in his ear, "Please give me ten minutes to live!" "No more than ten!" replied Bluebeard.
The girl ran to her sister Anna, who had gone up to one of the towers and asked her, "Anna, do you see our brothers coming? They promised to come and see me today!"
"No, I don't see anyone. What's wrong?" asked Anna.
"Anna, please," said the shaken girl, "look again! Are you sure you can't see anyone?"
"No," said her sister. Just then Bluebeard's voice boomed up at them, "Wife, your time is up! Come here!"

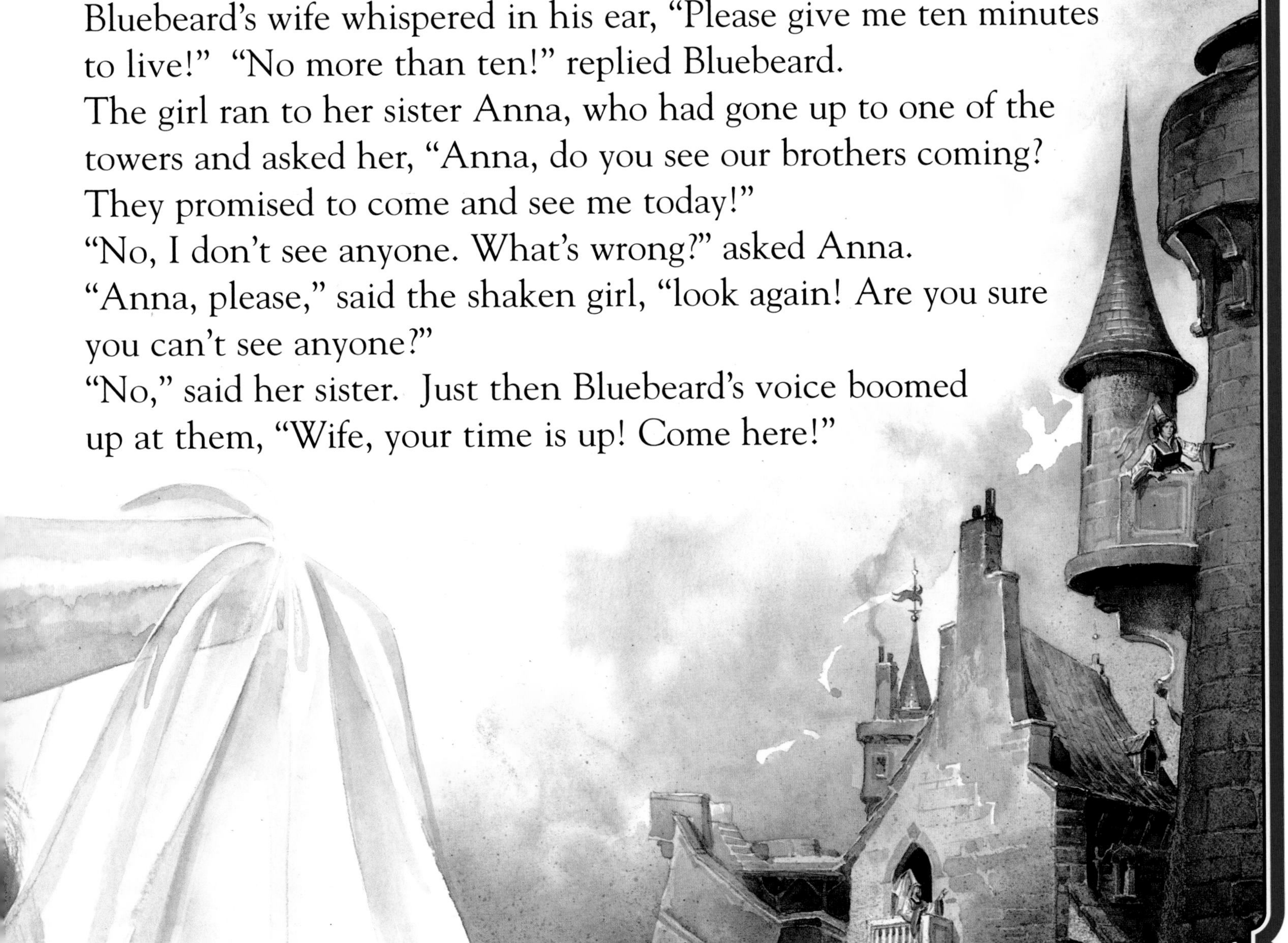

"I'm coming!" she called. Then she said to her sister, "Oh, Anna, aren't our brothers coming?"

"No," replied Anna.

"Come down at once!" shouted Bluebeard. Trembling like a leaf, his wife went downstairs. Bluebeard was now clutching a big knife!

"Sister, I see two horsemen coming!" called Anna from the tower.
"They too will die!" screamed Bluebeard.
"Please don't kill me. I'll never tell anyone what I saw!" pleaded his wife.
"You must die!" he replied fiercely. He was about to bring the knife down on the girl's neck, when two young men burst into the room. They were his wife's brothers.
Drawing their swords, they leapt towards Bluebeard, and killed him. And that was the end of the sad story.
Bluebeard's poor wives were given a proper burial. Some time later, the young widow married a good and honest young man, who helped her to forget her terrible adventure.

Fairy Tales from the FAR EAST

The Thousand and One Nights **-** This is the most famous collection of tales from the Far East, and includes such stories as "Ali Baba" and "Aladdin." However, it may be surprising to know that no one is exactly sure when these tales were written, and by whom. The one aspect they all have in common is that of a "frame story": the setting is central Asia, and a young wife, in order to convince her husband, the king, to spare her life, tells him a story, always promising to finish it the next night. In the end, the king enjoys the stories and he lets his wife live.

A Mixture of Backgrounds - The main characters' names are Persian, but the greatest number of names are Arabic. The frame story seems to be from India, but the tales take place in many countries, including: India, Egypt, Iran, Iraq, Turkey, and Greece. The stories, most likely dating anywhere from the 12th to the 16th century, originated as oral tales.

Directly above, an odalisk (female slave) dances. Right, scene from an Arabian city: camel drivers, men selling water, and a market with musicians.

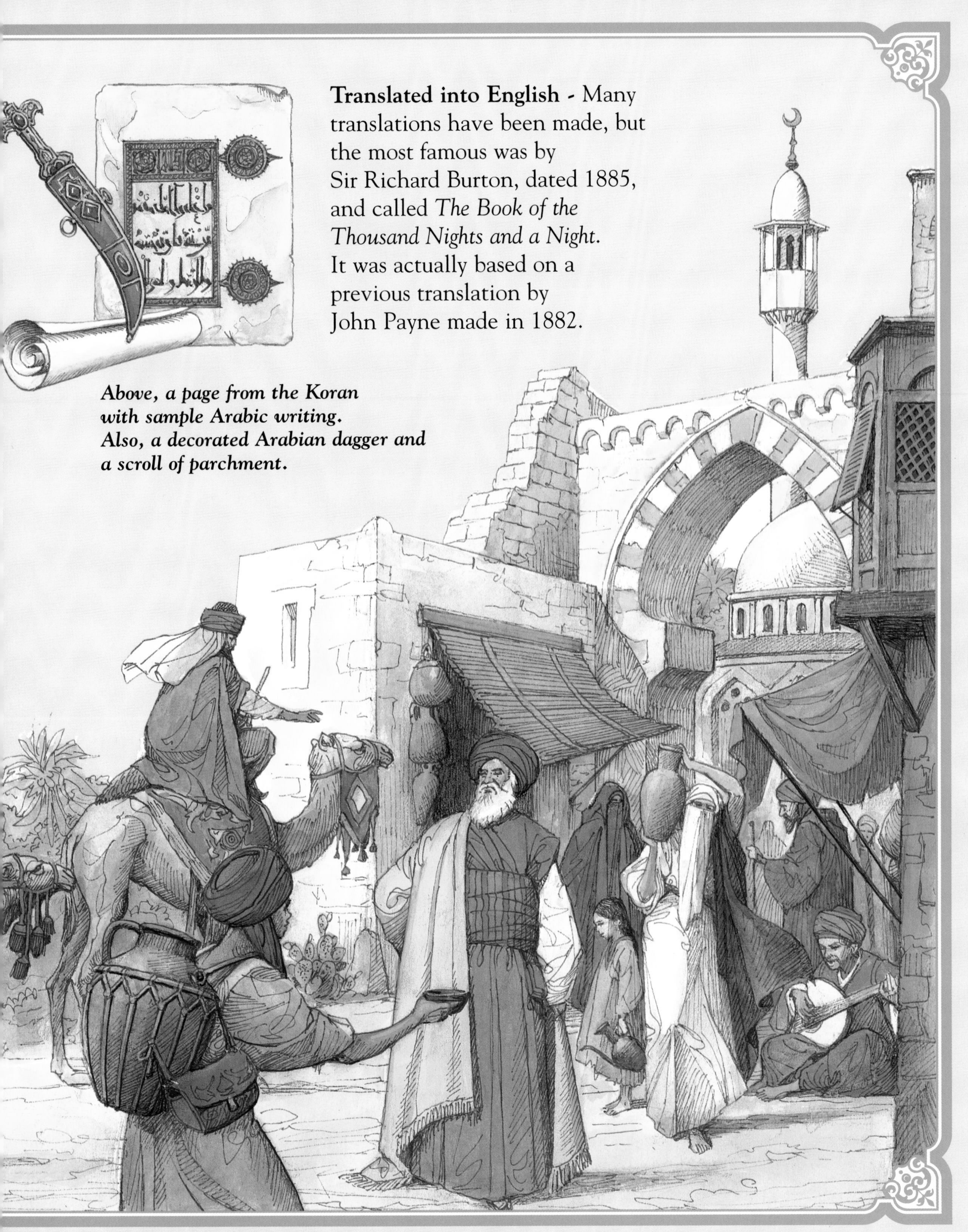

Translated into English - Many translations have been made, but the most famous was by Sir Richard Burton, dated 1885, and called *The Book of the Thousand Nights and a Night*. It was actually based on a previous translation by John Payne made in 1882.

Above, a page from the Koran with sample Arabic writing. Also, a decorated Arabian dagger and a scroll of parchment.

The Adventures of Aladdin

Once upon a time . . . a widow had an only son whose name was Aladdin. They were very poor and lived from hand to mouth. Aladdin did what he could to earn some pennies by picking bananas in faraway places.

One day, as he was looking for wild figs in a grove some way from the town, Aladdin met a mysterious stranger. The smartly dressed man asked Aladdin an unusual question:
"How would you like to earn a silver penny?"
"A silver penny!" exclaimed Aladdin. "Sir, I'll do anything!"
"Just go down that manhole. I'm much too big to squeeze through myself. If you do as I ask, you'll have your reward."
Slim and agile, the boy went down easily. His feet touched stone and he carefully made his way down some steps . . .

. . . and found himself in a large cave. The flickering light of an old oil lamp shone on a wonderful sight: trees dripping with glittering jewels, pots of gold, and chests full of priceless gems. It was a treasure-trove! Unable to believe his eyes, Aladdin was standing dazed when he heard a shout behind him.

"The lamp! Put out the flame and bring me the lamp!"

"Why would he want only an old lamp?" wondered Aladdin. "He must be a wizard!"

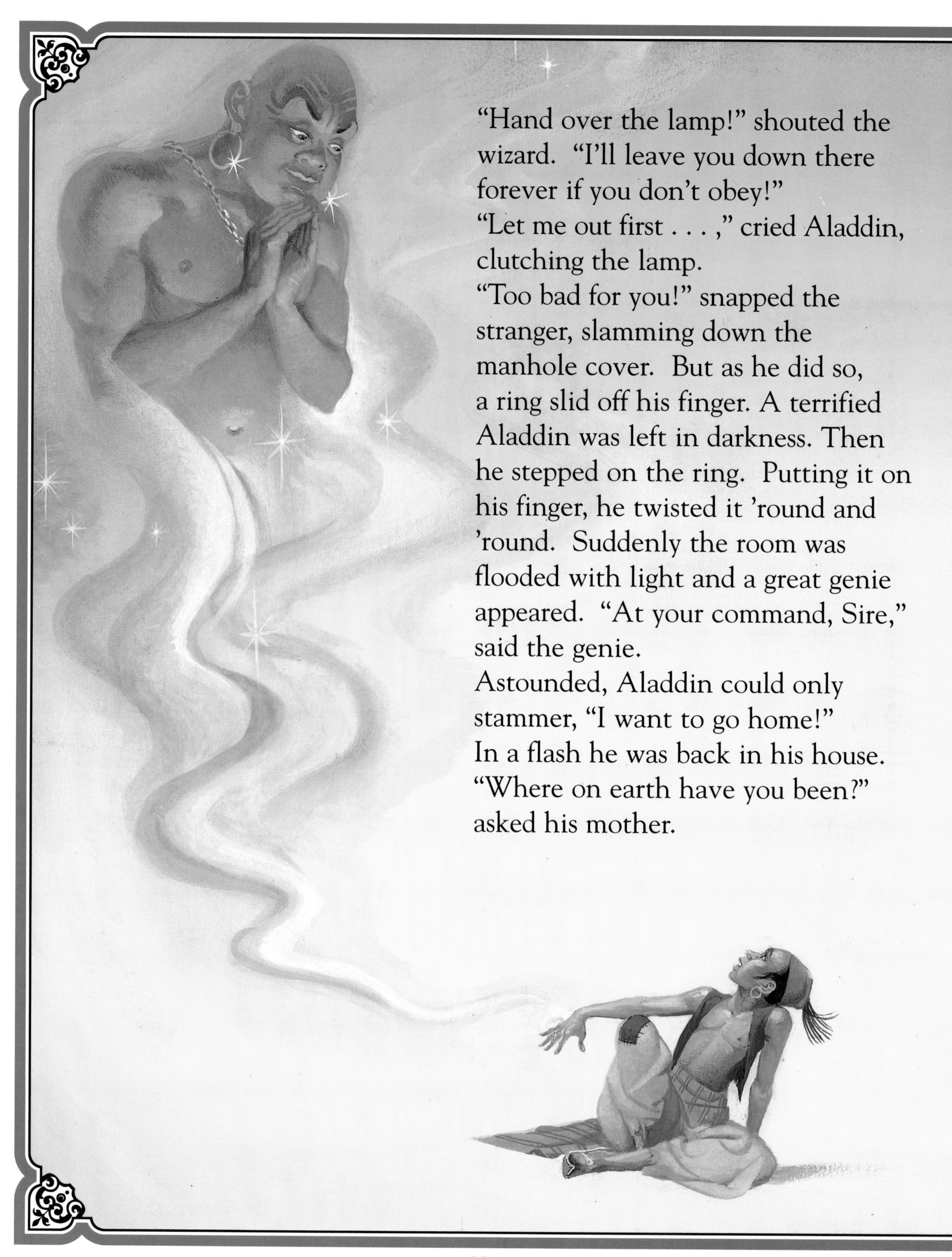

"Hand over the lamp!" shouted the wizard. "I'll leave you down there forever if you don't obey!"
"Let me out first . . . ," cried Aladdin, clutching the lamp.
"Too bad for you!" snapped the stranger, slamming down the manhole cover. But as he did so, a ring slid off his finger. A terrified Aladdin was left in darkness. Then he stepped on the ring. Putting it on his finger, he twisted it 'round and 'round. Suddenly the room was flooded with light and a great genie appeared. "At your command, Sire," said the genie.
Astounded, Aladdin could only stammer, "I want to go home!"
In a flash he was back in his house.
"Where on earth have you been?" asked his mother.

Excitedly, Aladdin told her of his adventures. Then he showed her the oil lamp. "Well, I hope it works. It's so dirty . . . ," she said, rubbing the lamp. Suddenly, in a cloud of smoke, out shot another genie. "I'm your obedient servant. Tell me your wishes," said the genie, bowing respectfully. The boy and his mother stared wordlessly at the incredible apparition.

"I'm here at your command. Tell me what you want," repeated the genie.

Aladdin gulped, then said,

"Bring us . . . a lovely big meal."

From that day on, Aladdin and his mother had everything they could wish for: food, clothes, and a fine home. The genie of the lamp granted them everything they asked for.

Aladdin soon grew into a tall, handsome young man and his mother felt it was time he found himself a wife.

One day, Aladdin happened to see the Sultan's daughter, Halima, being carried through the streets. He only caught a glimpse of the princess, but it was enough for him to want to marry her. Aladdin told his mother and she quickly said, "I'll go ask the Sultan for his daughter's hand." She arrived at the palace with a chest full of big diamonds for the Sultan.

"If Aladdin wants to marry Halima," said the Sultan, "he must send me forty slaves. Every slave must bring a box of precious stones, and forty warriors must escort the treasure."

Aladdin's mother went home.
When Aladdin heard the news, he picked up the lamp, rubbed it harder than ever and told the genie what he required.
The genie clapped his hands three times.
Forty slaves magically appeared, carrying the gemstones, and escorted by forty warriors.
When the Sultan saw all of this, he accepted Aladdin as his daughter's bridegroom.
But then he told Aladdin that he had to build a splendid palace for Halima.
Aladdin went straight home and asked the genie to build him a grand palace, which the genie did immediately.
The wedding then took place, with great celebrations.
News of Aladdin's fortunes and wealth spread like wildfire . . .

. . . until one day, a strange merchant stopped beneath the palace windows.
"Old lamps for new!" he called to the princess. Now, Aladdin had never told Halima about the lamp's secret powers. Wanting to surprise Aladdin, Halima fetched the old oil lamp and exchanged it for a new one. The merchant quickly began to rub it . . . and the genie was at the service of the wizard, who had his magic lamp back.

In a second he whisked away all of Aladdin's possessions and sent the palace and the princess to an unknown land.
Aladdin and the Sultan were at their wits' end. Nobody knew what had happened. Then, Aladdin remembered the genie of the ring. Slipping the ring on his finger, Aladdin twisted it 'round and 'round.

“Take me to the place where the wizard has hidden my wife,” he ordered the genie. In a flash, he found himself inside his own palace, and from behind a curtain, he saw the wizard and the princess, now his servant.

“Psst! Psst!” hissed Aladdin.

“Aladdin! It’s you!”

“Ssh . . . don’t let him hear you. Take this powder and put it in his tea.” The powder quickly took effect and the wizard fell into a deep sleep.

Aladdin hunted for the lamp high and low. He found it, at last, underneath the wizard’s pillow. He rubbed it hastily.

“Welcome back, Master! I’m glad to see you again. What can I do for you?” said the smiling genie.

“First, put this wicked wizard in chains and send him far away where he’ll never be found,” ordered Aladdin.

The genie grinned with pleasure, nodded his head, and the wizard vanished. Halima clutched Aladdin in fear. "What's going on? Who is that genie?" she asked.
"Don't worry, everything is all right," Aladdin reassured her. Then he told his wife the whole story from the beginning. The happy pair hugged each other.
"Can we return to our own kingdom?" the princess asked, thinking of her father.
"The magic that brought you here will take you back, but with me at your side, forever," replied Aladdin.

Meanwhile, the Sultan was ill with worry. Everyone had lost all hope of ever seeing the two again, when from far away, Aladdin rubbed the magic lamp and said, "Take my wife, me, and the palace back to our own land."

"In a flash, Sire," replied the genie. At the snap of a finger, the palace rose into the air and sped over the Sultan's kingdom.

It gently floated down to earth and landed on its old site. Aladdin and Halima rushed to embrace the Sultan.

To this very day, in that distant country, you can still admire the traces of an ancient palace which folk call "the palace that came from the skies."

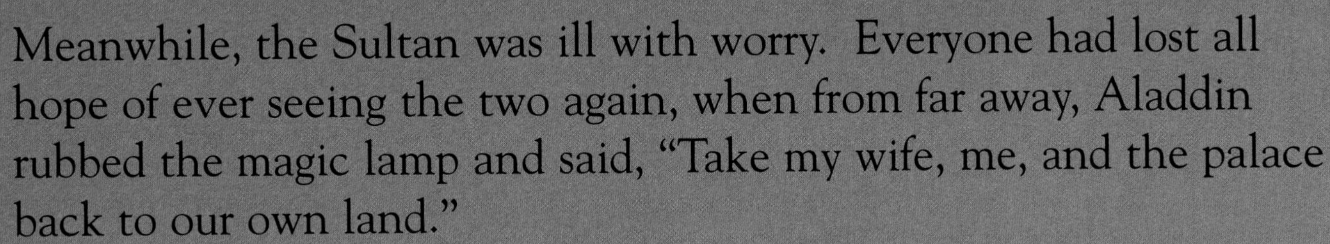

Ali Baba and the Forty Thieves

Once upon a time . . . in a distant Persian city lived two brothers called Ali Baba and Kasim. Ali Baba was terribly poor. He lived with his wife in a mud hut, and picked up sticks to sell in the market. Kasim had a rich wife and lived in a fine house.

One day, as Ali Baba was gathering sticks some way from the city, he heard a band of horsemen galloping toward him.
He scrambled up a tree and hid in the foliage, seconds before a group of armed men rode underneath.
Ali Baba could tell by their evil looks that the men were dangerous, but when he saw them unloading booty from their horses, he knew they were thieves. Their leader, a grim-faced man, strode toward the base of a nearby rocky hill.
"Open Sesame!" he shouted, throwing his arms wide.
Ali Baba could hardly believe his eyes. At the thief's words, the rock face swung open to become the entrance to a dark cave.
The robbers trooped inside, dragging their sacks.
Not daring to move a muscle, Ali Baba crouched in his tree.

He heard the robbers' voices echoing in the cave, then out they came. Ali Baba counted them: there were forty thieves in all! "Close Sesame!" cried the leader. The rock swung tightly shut as the robbers leapt onto their horses and galloped away.
Trembling with fear, Ali Baba climbed down the tree. He said, "Open Sesame," but the rock remained still. So, Ali Baba shouted "Open Sesame!" The rock began to move. Ali Baba lit a torch and stepped over the threshold of the cave. What a sight met his eyes! There were piles of treasure — gold and silver bowls, weapons studded with rubies and emeralds, twinkling coins, and richly hued carpets. He picked up a coin, his hand shaking like a leaf.
"It's real!" he gasped, stunned at such untold wealth.

"I'll take some coins — nobody will ever know," Ali Baba thought, filling four bags full. When he reached home he locked the door and emptied the sacks in front of his astounded wife.
They started counting them. But there were far too many coins. "We can't count them all," said Ali Baba finally. "Run to my brother's house and ask for a corn measure."
When Kasim's wife heard this strange request, her curiosity was aroused. "I wonder what they want to measure. It can't be corn, they're far too poor." And she quickly brushed a touch of tar across the bottom of the measure. When she got it back, something was stuck to it: a gold coin!
She rushed off to tell her husband.
Kasim was annoyed. "How dare my brother have gold coins without informing me?" he cried.
Ali Baba innocently told Kasim his strange story, but asked him to keep it a secret.

Kasim promised, but quickly told his wife.

He ordered the servants to saddle ten sturdy mules for the next morning. All night long he lay awake thinking of the treasure.

It was still dark when Kasim and his mule train set out.

When he reached the rock, he said the magic words and entered the cave. With beating heart, he crammed as much as he could into the saddle bags. They soon became too heavy to lift, and he realized he would have to leave some things behind.

He was still picking over his treasure when, unluckily for Kasim, the forty thieves returned. When they saw the entrance to the cave wide open, they drew their swords and rushed in. Poor Kasim was quickly discovered and slain. The ferocious robbers cut his body into quarters and left it at the entrance to the cave.

"That should warn off any others!" shouted the leader.

Kasim's wife waited for two days, then she ran to Ali Baba and told him where her husband had gone, asking for help. Ali Baba, fond of his brother, was dismayed at the news.
He saddled a mule and rode to the rock. When he saw Kasim's remains, he wept. Finally he wrapped the remains in a rug, which he tied to the mule's back.
The shock was too great for Kasim's wife, who died of a broken heart. Ali Baba and his family went to live in Kasim's palace.

Among the servants of the palace was Morgantina, a clever young slave girl. She told Ali Baba that his brother's remains could be put together again before being buried. Mustapha, the cobbler, would do it for a good reward.

"I'll have to blindfold you for the journey," the slave told Mustapha. The cobbler did his work well and was paid a bag of gold for his trouble. He was led, again blindfolded, back to his shop.

Meanwhile, the robber leader had returned to find Kasim's body gone. He knew that someone else had found the treasure. Angry, he sent one of his men to the city to find out what he could.

By chance, the spy stopped at the cobbler's shop. Mustapha was bursting to tell someone about his good luck. ". . . And they gave me a bag of gold for stitching the body together," he recalled.

"If you take me to the place, I'll give you another bag of gold," said the robber. The cobbler's heart sank. How was he to find the house again?

"I'll blindfold you," said the

robber, "then you can take your time and try to remember."
Mustapha, although blindfolded, had taken the precaution of counting his steps. He counted them again: "Five hundred and ten — eleven — twelve — Here!" The cobbler wrenched the blindfold off. They were standing in front of Ali Baba's palace.
The robber handed Mustapha a bag of gold and, unseen, drew a red cross on the door. He hurried off to tell his leader the news.
Dusk fell, and as Morgantina was about to enter the palace, she noticed the strange mark. Suspicious, she quickly drew a red cross on all the other doors on the street.

When the forty thieves arrived to take revenge they stopped in their tracks. Which was the right house?
"Fools!" cried the enraged robber chief. "Can't you do anything?"
The next day he went to Mustapha's shop disguised as a merchant. The cobbler was only too delighted to earn more gold, and took the chief to Ali Baba's door as before.
The robber chief returned to his hideout and ordered two of his men to buy a large cart and forty giant oil jars. Each of the robbers hid in a jar, except for the chief, who again disguised himself as a merchant. The last jar was filled with oil and loaded onto the cart with the others. It was late when they reached the palace. Ali Baba himself came out. "What can I do for you?" he asked.
"I am an oil merchant," replied the chief. "It's late and I'm weary. Can you give me a bed for the night?"

Ali Baba welcomed the merchant, had his cart taken into the courtyard, and offered him a hearty meal. After dinner, the chief said he wanted to make sure none of the oil jars had been damaged on the journey. He went from jar to jar, whispering to his men to be ready at his signal, and then to attack and kill everyone.

As the household slept, Morgantina finished her work in the kitchen. "I wonder if the merchant's oil tastes better than ours . . . ," she said to herself, and went out to the courtyard. But when she lifted the lid from the first jar, a gruff voice said, "Is it time yet?"

"No, not yet," replied Morgantina hastily. At every jar, exactly the same thing happened, but the last one was filled with oil. This she dragged back to the kitchen. She poured the oil into a cauldron and heated it over the fire. Then she tiptoed from jar to jar in the courtyard, pouring boiling oil over every one of the robbers.

She hid in a corner to wait. A little later, the robber chief crept into the courtyard to give the signal. But when he raised the lids, he found that all his men were dead. Terrified, he fled into the night.

The next morning, Morgantina told Ali Baba of her adventure. "I'll never be able to thank you enough!" exclaimed her master. "You are an amazing girl. From this moment on, you are no longer a slave, but a free member of this household."

Meanwhile, the robber chief, eager for revenge, shaved off his beard and disguised himself as a carpet seller. At the market he met Tabit, Ali Baba's son, who took a liking to him. "Sooner or later, this silly boy will invite me to his father's home," said the chief to himself, "and then I can murder them all."

"That merchant sold you very fine carpets very cheaply," remarked Ali Baba to his son; "Ask him to the house."

As Morgantina served refreshments,

she felt sure the guest looked familiar. She realized with a shiver that the carpet seller was the robber chief. Morgantina asked if she could dance for the guest. "If you like," said Ali Baba. When coffee was served, Morgantina entered in a swirl of veils, beating her tambourine. In her right hand she held a knife. As she stopped dancing, she plunged the knife into the carpet seller's heart. "What have you done?" gasped Ali Baba. "He's the robber chief!" cried Morgantina. "I know his face. He would have murdered us all!"

Once again Morgantina had saved the day! In the end, Ali Baba was the only one who knew the magic words that would open the cave of the forty thieves, but he decided never, ever to tell anyone else.

The Ruby Prince

Once upon a time . . . a beggar in faraway Persia had a stroke of luck. After a sudden flood, the river near the capital city shrank back to its old size, leaving mud behind it on the banks. In the mud, the beggar caught sight of a sparkling red stone. He picked it up and hurried off to see one of his friends who worked in the royal kitchens.

"How many dinners would you give me for this shining stone?" he asked the man hopefully.

"But this is a ruby!" exclaimed the cook. "You must take it to the Shah!" So, the next day, the beggar took the stone to the Shah, who asked him, "Where did you find this?"

"Lying in the mud on the bank of the river, Sire!" he said.

"Hmm!" mused the Shah. "Now why did the great river leave such a treasure to you? I'll give you a bag of gold for the stone. Will that do?"

The beggar could scarcely believe his ears.
"Sire, this is the most wonderful day of my life,"
he stammered. "My humblest thanks!"
Before the Shah locked the big stone in his treasure chest, he called to his daughter Fatima and said, "This is the biggest ruby I've ever seen. I shall give it to you for your eighteenth birthday!"

Fatima threw her arms around her father's neck.

"It's marvelous! Thank you. It will bring me good luck!"

Some months later, on Fatima's birthday, the Shah went to fetch the ruby. But when he lifted the lid of the chest, he leapt in surprise, for out stepped a handsome young man who said, "The ruby you want no longer exists! I've taken its place. I am the Ruby Prince. Please don't ask how this miracle took place. It's a secret I can never tell!" When the Shah got over his shock, he went into a rage. "I lose a precious gem, find a prince, and I'm not allowed to ask the reason why?" he roared.

"I'm sorry, Sire," replied the Prince, "but nothing and nobody will make me tell how I got here."
Furious, the Shah decided to punish the young man.
"Since you've taken the place of my ruby," he thundered, "you are now my servant, I presume."
"Of course, Sire," replied the young man confidently.
"Good!" exclaimed the Shah. "Then take my golden sword.
I'll reward you with the hand of my daughter, Fatima, if you succeed in killing the dragon of the Valley of Death that is preventing the caravans from passing through the forest."
As it was, many a brave young man had lost his life trying to kill the terrible dragon, and the Shah was quite sure that the Ruby Prince would share their fate. Armed with the Shah's sword, the Ruby Prince set off for the Valley of Death.

When he reached the edge of the forest, he called out for the dragon to show itself. But the only reply was the echo of his own voice. He sat down to rest, when the sound of snapping branches brought him to his feet. There was a very loud hissing and the earth trembled. The dragon was before him. The horrible beast reared with open jaws. But the Prince stoutly stood his ground. He struck first one heavy blow and then another, until the monster lay dead.

When he returned to the palace carrying the dragon's head, the Ruby Prince was hailed as a hero. And so Fatima and the Ruby Prince were married and lived happily together. However, as time passed, Fatima became curious about her husband's past. "I know nothing about you," she complained. "At least tell me who you really are and where you once lived!" But every time the Ruby Prince heard such remarks, he said, "I cannot tell you. You must not ask, or you will run the risk of losing me forever!"

But Fatima was tormented by the desire to know. One day, as they sat by the river that flowed through the Shah's gardens, Fatima pleaded with him to reveal his secret. The Ruby Prince hesitated, gazing at his dear wife and gently stroking her hair. Then he made his decision: "I don't want to see you suffer like this. If you really must know, then I'll tell you that I am —" At the very second he was to reveal his secret, a huge wave swept him into the river and he disappeared under the water.

The princess rushed along the bank, crying loudly for her husband, but he had vanished. Fatima called the guards and even the Shah himself ran to comfort her. But the princess was very sad, for she knew that her foolish questioning had been the cause of the tragedy. One day, her handmaiden said, "Your Highness! I saw the most amazing sight last night. A host of tiny lights appeared on the river, then a thousand little genies draped the river bank with flowers. A handsome young man began to dance in honor of an old man, a king. Beside the king stood a young man with a ruby on his forehead." Fatima's heart leaped. Could the young man with the ruby be her husband? That night, the princess went into the garden and hid behind a tree. At midnight, lights began to twinkle on the river and an old man holding a scepter rose from the water, followed by a young man. Fatima recognized her husband. Covering her face with her veil, she left her hiding place and began to dance.

Wild applause greeted her at the end. Then from the throne came a voice: "For such a divine dance, tell us your wish and it will be granted!"

Fatima cried, "Give me back my husband!"

The old king rose and said, "The King of the Waters of Persia has given his word. Take back the Ruby Prince. But be wiser in the future!" Then the waters opened once more and closed over the king and his court, leaving Fatima and the Ruby Prince on the bank, reunited and happy at last.

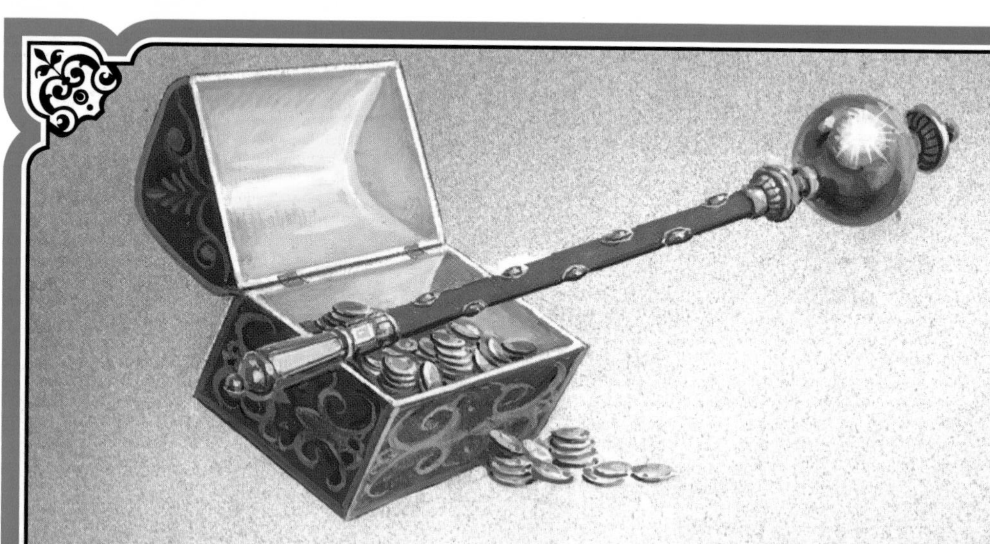

The Weeping Princess

Once upon a time . . . a greedy emperor forced his subjects to pay heavy taxes. Not only were the poor affected — the nobles in the empire were highly taxed, too. Tired of this, they held a protest meeting. When the emperor heard about it, he feared a rebellion. So he sent out a proclamation: "The nobleman that can make my daughter Sarah smile will never, ever have to pay taxes again."

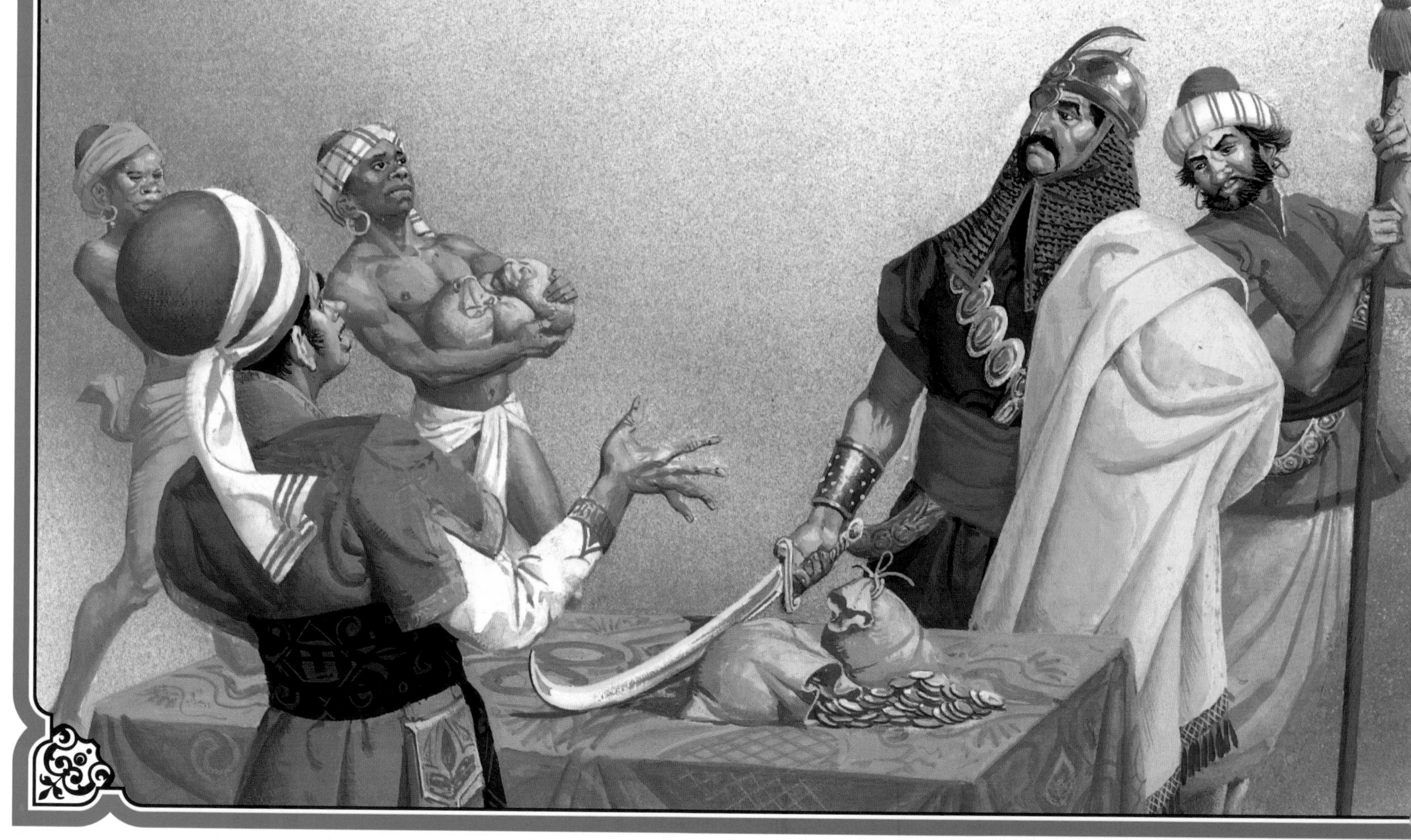

This caused an uproar at the meeting. The nobles were very skeptical, and pointed out that the emperor had not abolished any taxes. Most of the princes, however, did not complain; each was sure he would succeed, and left to begin his preparations.
From that day on, noble knights came to the palace from all over the empire to try and console the weeping princess. Crowds cheered them as they passed, but booed and whistled at them when they returned, heads bowed in failure.
The days went by and the list of defeated knights grew longer. Indians, Circassians, Arabs, and Turks from all of the provinces came. They were bold young men filled with confidence, but when the princess saw them, she wept uncontrollably.
The emperor was delighted, because each failure meant another taxpayer.
Even the common folk seemed contented; they saw that the rich did not always succeed.
The only unhappy person was Sarah, who continued to weep.

One day, a Mongol prince seemed to be about to win a smile from Sarah. He strummed his balalaika for hours, playing everything from sad tunes to merry jigs. The princess stared at him, dry-eyed, and the onlookers thought she was about to smile, when she burst into tears. A Kurdish chief, famed for his humor and for keeping the courts in fits of laughter, tried to make Sarah smile with his witty remarks. But her dark eyes filled with tears.

Noblemen came from as far away as Persia, but in vain. The only person who had not yet appeared was Omar, the chief of a very tiny province far, far away from the palace. A bright and intelligent young man, he had outwitted certain greedy relatives who had tried to remove his power when he succeeded his uncle as chief. The emperor's messengers had taken a long time to reach this remote land. Although Omar set out at once, he had to ride for many days on his fine black horse. Then one evening, he reached the palace. When the dusty traveler explained to the stable boys why he had come, they laughed in scorn.

But they had to obey orders, so they told him to enter. "It is late, so you will not see the princess until tomorrow," they said.

The emperor's other daughters, however, were soon told of the new arrival. "He is the most handsome of them all!" they exclaimed.

The next morning, the emperor ordered the newcomer to be led before Sarah. The court crowded around to watch. Unlike all of the other suitors, Omar did nothing at all to amuse the princess. He stared at Sarah without saying a word, and she stared back with an empty look on her face.

Then Omar went back to the emperor and said, "Sire! Give me your scepter and I will solve the problem of Sarah!" Surprised at such an odd request, the emperor gave him the scepter. The other princesses clustered around, admiring the handsome young man. First he made a deep bow to Sarah, then he straightened up and dealt her a blow on the head with the scepter. Screams filled the air; the emperor threw up his arms in rage and his daughters fled in all directions. The guards drew their swords. Then the whole room stopped in

amazement, for out of Sarah's head rolled broken springs and pieces of metal. The princess who had never smiled was a doll! And no one had even realized this, except for Omar.

The emperor's youngest daughter, Marika, could not stop laughing. The emperor glared at her. "Be quiet!" he ordered. But the emperor saw the humor in this as well. For he had been making use of Sarah the doll to guarantee a steady flow of taxes from all of his subjects. And now, a man more cunning had exposed his trick. The emperor suddenly had a very good idea. To Omar he said, "You should be put to death for this insolence, but, I will spare your life if you marry my youngest daughter. Of course, you won't have to pay any taxes."

Omar nodded as he smiled at Marika, who was very happy.

Behind his smile, Omar was thinking, "Dear father-in-law, one day I will be sitting on your throne!" And just a few years later, he was.

The Adventures of Sayed

Once upon a time . . . in the mysterious East, lived a man, Benezar, who married a woman, Zemira. They were in love and agreed on all things, except one. Zemira believed in magic, while Benezar only believed in what he could see. However, that did not mar their happiness, and one day, during a thunderstorm, Zemira gave birth to a handsome baby boy. When Benezar was allowed to see the baby, he noticed a tiny whistle hanging from a thin silver thread around his neck. "What's this?" he asked.

"It's a gift from a fairy to our son," replied Zemira. "It's a magic gift. Take it," she said, removing the

whistle, "and give it to our son when he is twenty."
"All right. But tell me, what are we to call the child?" asked Benezar.
"Sayed," replied Zemira.
The years went by and Sayed grew healthy, strong, and brave. He was eighteen years old when he decided to go on a pilgrimage to the holy city of Mecca. "I am pleased that you are going," said Benezar. "Sayed, take this as a lucky charm," and he gave his son the fairy's gift.
"What is it?" Sayed asked. "It's a whistle. Your mother, alas now dead, said to carry it with you always," replied his father.
"I will," said the young man, putting the whistle around his neck.
Not long after, the travelers set out on their journey.

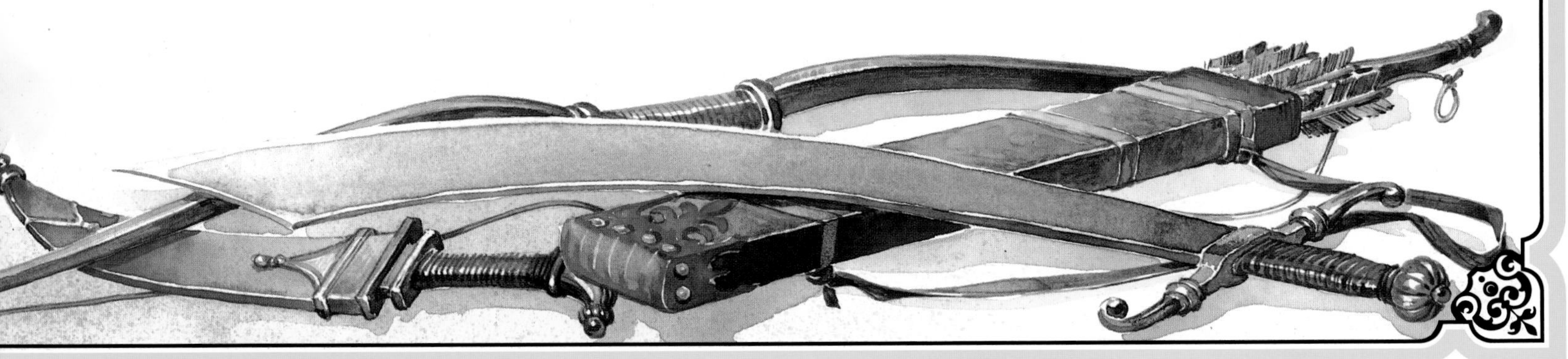

Young Sayed was splendidly equipped, armed with a sword, spear, and bow and arrows. It was a long way to the holy city of Mecca. They traveled over plains, mountains, and deserts. On a long stretch of desert they were attacked by a large band of robbers. Caught unaware, some tried to flee, but Sayed shouted, "Flee? To where? We will die fighting!" and he hurled himself into the fray.
During the fighting, Sayed was attacked by a young robber on a white horse. He bravely faced him and killed him with his sword. A nearby soldier shouted, "What have you done? You've killed Almansor. This is the end! Run!" Men ran in all directions. Alone, Sayed remembered the whistle. He put it to his lips and blew hard, but nothing happened.
So, Sayed was taken prisoner and led before Sheik Selim, a powerful man who was the leader of several of the desert tribes and the father of Almansor, the man Sayed had killed.
Selim, however, was not an unjust man. When he discovered that Almansor had died in a fair fight, he refused to allow any harm to come to Sayed. Indeed, he set him free and entrusted the young man to some travelers leaving for Mecca.

Sayed traveled on, but one night friends of Almansor captured him. "Your master Selim told you not to kill me," cried the young man. "We're not going to kill you. We're going to tie you up and leave you here in the desert. Thirst, the sun, the vultures, and jackals will do the rest!" And they rode off. Two whole days went by. Sayed was on the verge of dying, when some travelers

working for Kalum, the merchant, passed nearby. They came to Sayed's aid and saved his life. Later, when he came to his senses, Sayed said, "May Allah reward you, sir, for saving my life. What is your name?" "My name is Kalum," said the man, "but it won't be Allah who will reward me; you will. You are going to work for me until you have repaid that debt. What is your name?"

"Sayed," he answered.

"Well, Sayed, come with me."

The young man went with Kalum and discovered that he was a rich merchant from Baghdad. At that time, Baghdad was ruled by the famous Caliph, Harun-el-Rashid,

who was wise, and loved by all. Kalum owned a big bazaar in the city and it was there that Sayed worked, doing humble jobs. One day, a veiled woman came to the bazaar. Sayed was amazed when she said to him, "You're Sayed, aren't you?"

"Yes!" he replied in astonishment. "How did you know that?"

"Tell me, have you still got the whistle around your neck?" she asked.

"Of course!" said the young man. "You must be the fairy! What is it for?" The woman responded, "It will be of no use until you are twenty. Then it will save your life. Now, what can I do for you?"

"Help me to get home," Sayed replied. "I need lots of money."

"You're brave and strong. You can earn it," said the woman, and she explained that every week, tournaments were held in the city. The Caliph always watched and the winners received prizes. The veiled woman had weapons, armor, and horses and she lent these to Sayed. He took part in the tournaments and won many prizes, as well as the Caliph's admiration. Sayed, however, never revealed his name; he only said he was a horseman from Cairo.

The Caliph liked to wander the city at night, disguised as a beggar, to hear what folk had to say. One night, as Sayed was going home, he heard the sounds of struggle. Four men had attacked two others. Sayed immediately came to the rescue, killing two of the attackers and chasing the others away. The two victims thanked Sayed and asked him what his name was. "My name is Sayed," came the reply. "I'm Kalum the merchant's shop assistant."

"You seem to be more of a gentleman than a shop assistant," said one of the men. "Take this ring as a reward."

The other man said, "And this bag of coins. You've saved my life!" Sayed stood with the ring and bag in his hand. With these he could find a ship and go home.

The next day, Sayed told Kalum that he was leaving.
"And where are you going to?" asked Kalum.
"Home!" said Sayed.
"But it's a costly journey and with the wages I pay you —"
Sayed smiled. "Your pay wouldn't take me far, but . . . ," and he held out the bag, "this money will. Farewell!"
However, wicked Kalum was not to be defeated. He told the police Sayed had stolen a bag of gold and the young man was arrested. The police asked, "Who gave you this money?"
"A man I'd never seen before," was the honest reply. Sayed was judged a thief and deported to Thirsty Island, with the worst criminals.
The young man thought, "I left home two years ago, proud, rich, and happy. Here I am, twenty years old, condemned to die an innocent man in prison!" That night there was a storm, and the ship traveling to Thirsty Island was flung about until it crashed onto some rocks.

Only one man survived the disaster: Sayed. At the mercy of the waters, he groped for something to hold on to, until he touched the whistle. Desperately, he blew it . . . and a dolphin surfaced beside him. Sayed rode it to safety. As the fairy had said, when he was twenty years old, the whistle would save his life!
The dolphin carried the young man within sight of land. "Thank you, friend!" called out Sayed as he slid down and swam ashore.

To his surprise, there was a military camp. Sayed was taken prisoner and brought before none other than Harun-el-Rashid himself.
The soldiers said, "Sire, this man is one of the convicts. He must have survived the shipwreck."
"Is that so?" Harun-el-Rashid demanded gravely.
"Yes," replied Sayed, "I did survive the shipwreck. But I'm not a convict." He explained about the bag of gold. "It was given to me," he went on, "by one of two men I saved." Harun-el-Rashid glanced at his minister and said, "Did the two men give you anything else?"
"Yes, they did: this ring," Sayed replied, showing the Caliph the ring which he kept around his neck. Harun exclaimed, "Young man, the two men you helped were my chief minister and myself! Go free, but first . . . tell me your name once again."
"Sayed, Sire." "Sayed?" echoed the chief minister. "There's a man here in the camp called Benezar, who is searching for his son, Sayed."
"It's my father!" cried the young man.
Finding each other, Sayed and his father hugged in delight. In the end, justice prevailed and evil Kalum was arrested and imprisoned, as he deserved to be.

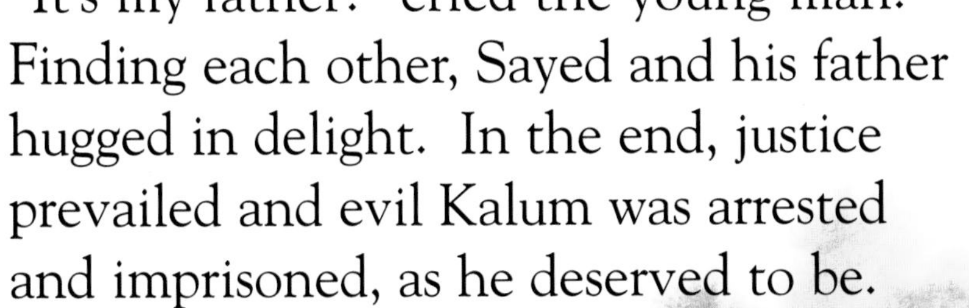

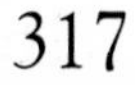

SALEM AND THE NAIL

Once upon a time . . . the shop belonging to an astute merchant named Salem, and all the carpets in it, burned in a fire. Salem was left with nothing but his house, and since he was a trader he decided to sell it. With the money he would be able to buy a new shop and more carpets. Salem did not ask a high price for his house. However, he had a most unusual request to make of would-be buyers: "I'll sell you the house, except for that nail in the wall. That remains mine!" They went off, shaking their heads and wondering what he meant by this strange remark. Abraham, however, was more miserly than the others. He thought the price was fair, and he haggled it down even further. A bargain was struck and the new owner took over the whole house, except for the nail.

A week later, Salem knocked on the door. "I've come to hang something on my nail," he said. Abraham let him in and Salem hung a large empty bag, said goodbye, and left. A few days later, he appeared again, and this time he hung an old cloak on the nail. From then on, Salem's visits became regular; he was forever coming and going, taking things off the nail or hanging something else up.

One evening, in front of the stunned eyes of Abraham and his family, Salem arrived dragging a dead donkey. With a struggle, he hoisted it up and tied it to the nail.

The occupants of the house complained about the smell and the sight of the dead beast, but Salem calmly said, "It's my nail and I can hang anything I like on it!"
Abraham, naturally, could no longer live in the house under such conditions. But Salem refused to remove the donkey.
"If you don't like it," he said, "you can get out of my house, but I'll not pay you back a penny!"
Abraham did his best to persuade Salem to take the donkey down, for it smelled to high heaven. He even consulted a judge, but the terms of the bargain were clear. The house belonged to Abraham, but Salem kept the nail.
In the end, Abraham was forced to leave and Salem got his house back without paying a penny for it!

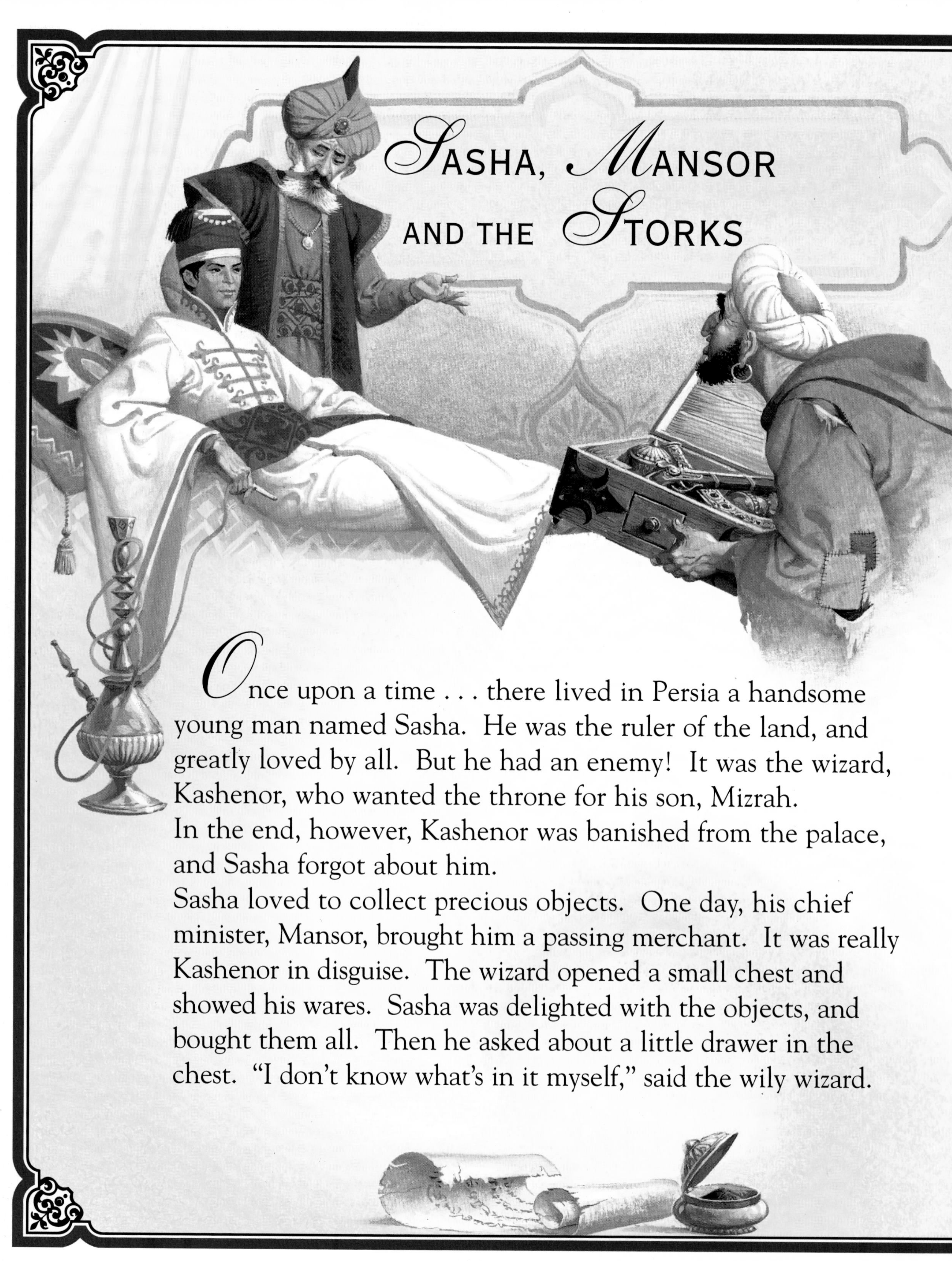

Sasha, Mansor and the Storks

Once upon a time . . . there lived in Persia a handsome young man named Sasha. He was the ruler of the land, and greatly loved by all. But he had an enemy! It was the wizard, Kashenor, who wanted the throne for his son, Mizrah.

In the end, however, Kashenor was banished from the palace, and Sasha forgot about him.

Sasha loved to collect precious objects. One day, his chief minister, Mansor, brought him a passing merchant. It was really Kashenor in disguise. The wizard opened a small chest and showed his wares. Sasha was delighted with the objects, and bought them all. Then he asked about a little drawer in the chest. "I don't know what's in it myself," said the wily wizard.

He opened the drawer and took out a jar full of black powder and a roll of old paper covered with strange writing. "Please, your Highness, take these as a gift," said the wizard, and he left. Sasha called his wise men to try to read the writing. After a few days, they had translated the words: "The man who reads these words will gain the power to become any animal he likes, and to know its language. All he must do is sniff the black powder and say the word MUTABOR. To become a man again, he must bow three times to the east and repeat the word." But the roll of paper also warned that the reader must never laugh in his animal shape or he would forget the magic word. "We can turn into animals, Mansor," cried the excited ruler. "Shall we try it?" "If that is your wish," replied Mansor, bowing low. At dawn the next day, Sasha and his minister went for a walk by a lake near the palace. They were wondering what animal to choose when a stork flew past. "Storks!" they cried. They sniffed the powder and said the word MUTABOR.

Their legs shrivelled into skinny limbs and their clothes turned into snowy feathers. Soon all trace of Sasha and his minister had vanished. How wonderful it was to be able to fly! The pair soared over the lake. "Let's find the other storks," said Sasha, and they headed down the river. When they saw a stork in shallow water, prancing around in its funny dance, they forgot all about the warning and began to laugh. As the afternoon wore on, they decided to fly back to the palace. They flapped slowly over the city. Something odd was going on: the streets were crowded, and a long procession was entering the palace gates. A stranger was sitting in Sasha's carriage, escorted by his own guards. "Who's that impostor?" cried Sasha. "It's Mizrah, the son of the banished wizard, Kashenor," said Mansor.

As he spoke, the minister shook with fear, for he realized he had forgotten the magic word. He looked at his master and saw that he, too, realized their plight. "We'll never be humans again!" said Mansor sadly. "Let us fly to Mecca and pray on the Prophet's tomb." But Mecca was a long way off, and the sun was setting. Tired and hungry, the two storks landed in the ruins of an old temple. As they looked around, they heard a dreadful screech. What was it? Sasha plucked up courage. "Let's find out. What have we got to lose?" he said. In a dark corner, the storks glimpsed the yellow eyes of a huge owl. When the creature saw them, it gave a mournful hoot, then spoke. "At last! The spell is sure to be broken after all these years."
Sasha and Mansor looked at each other in amazement.
"I am Naja, daughter of the King of India," said the owl. "The evil wizard, Kashenor

turned me into an owl when I refused to marry his son.
Then he exiled me to these ruins, saying I'd remain a bird until someone agreed to marry me."

"Kashenor again!" cried Sasha. He told the owl his story.

"Kashenor is dining here tonight with his fellow wizards," said the owl. "Perhaps he might boast of your disappearance, and repeat the magic word. But if I take you to him, will you promise to marry me?"

Sasha promised, and the owl quickly led the two storks to the banquet hall among the ruins.

Sure enough, Kashenor was there with his evil friends.

"Guess how I got rid of Sasha and that old fool Mansor?" boasted the wizard. Within seconds, he had pronounced the word MUTABOR.
"That's it!" cried the two storks joyfully, and hurried out of the ruins. They bowed three times to the east and said the magic word. Instantly they resumed their old forms.
The ruler and his minister hugged each other with relief. Then they turned to the owl . . .

. . . and what did they see but a beautiful princess in a silk sari and veil!
Sasha was entranced.
"You have my word," he assured the princess.
"We shall be married when I am on the throne again."
The three crept up to the wizards' camels and silently mounted them.
By dawn they had reached the city gates.

As they rode through the city, the street-sweepers began to shout. "It is our ruler, Sasha! He is alive!" Soon people gathered at windows and ran out of doors to see the ruler and his minister ride by with the beautiful princess. The citizens pressed around them, cheering wildly.

As soon as they reached the palace, Mansor sent the royal guards to capture Kashenor. Meanwhile, Sasha ordered the arrest of Mizrah. The wizard's son tried to escape, but it was too late.

The citizens were enraged when they discovered how Kashenor had tricked them. "Death! Put him to death!" cried the people.

The wicked Kashenor was executed. Mizrah was forced to sniff the black powder and say the word MUTABOR. He instantly turned into a stork, and was placed in a cage atop a high turret.

At last it was time for happier doings. Mansor organized a great feast, and Sasha, true to his word, married the beautiful Naja.

The Little Golden Bird

Once upon a time . . . several Buddhist monks lived in a great temple that stood in a magnificent garden. The monks spent their days contentedly in prayer and meditation, and the beauty of their surroundings made them forget the rest of the world.

Then one day a young monk arrived, telling them all about what lay beyond the garden wall. He told them about the cities, brightly lit and brimming with entertainment and pleasure. When the monks heard about the world outside, they no longer wanted to remain in what had, until then, seemed like paradise.

With the young monk as their leader, first one group then another left the temple. Weeds began to sprout on the paths and the temple seemed deserted. Slowly the last five monks, saddened by their love for the sacred spot, prepared to leave. But just as they turned their backs on the temple a golden bird, dangling five long white strings, fluttered over their heads. Each monk was drawn to clasp one of the strings, and the group found itself being carried away . . . and saw the outside world as it was, full of hate and violence; a world with no peace.

It was a long journey, and when the golden bird finally brought them back, they decided never to leave again. Three times the bird circled overhead, and the monks knew that Buddha had come to help them find true happiness.

Fairy Tales from RUSSIA

Ivan Andreyevich Krylov was born in 1768 in Moscow and died in 1844 in Saint Petersburg.

Animal Fables in Russian - In 1805, Krylov began translating the fables of La Fontaine into Russian. With this activity, he joined a long procession of fairy tale authors who were influenced by one another. In the end, Krylov found that he was better at writing his own fables, and he published his first book in 1809, containing twenty-three fables. He went on to write eight other books of fables, all in verse.

From Animal Tales to . . . Although Krylov borrowed some themes from Aesop and from La Fontaine, his characters and stories were actually very much of his own country. He wrote in a very simple but eloquent manner and was the first fairy tale author to become well-known by a great number of people throughout Russia. He actually had little formal education — nonetheless his writing was so good that many of his verses became famous proverbs.

Above, a scene from "The Prince and the Beggar."

Aleksander N. Afanasyev was born in 1826 in Boguchar, in the Voronezh Province, and died in 1871 in Moscow.

A Russian Collection . . . of fairy tales was begun by Afanasyev in 1855 and completed in 1864. Entitled *Russian Popular Fairy Tales*, it included hundreds and hundreds of tales, and became an important part of Russian literature. Afanasyev also wrote *Russian Popular Legends* but this book was banned until the year 1914. A theme common to Russian tales — the satire of members of the church or wealthy land-owners — is also found in his *Beloved Fairy Tales*. Written for children, the original publication of this book took place in Switzerland, under a pen name.

Below, Russia in the mid-1800s. Sleds were used to cover snowy ground. The noble-woman on the sled is attended to by her driver. The church is in the Russian Orthodox style. In the foreground, a grenadier speaks with a farmer.

Pictured at left: the manuscript of a religious book from the 1700s.

Above, Alex and Natasha from "Alex the Hunter." In this tale, Alex must believe what the fairy tells him, and doing so, he saves Natasha's life and his own.

Prince Ivan

Once upon a time . . . there was a valiant and kind prince named Ivan, who had a stepsister who was a witch. She disliked him very much, so much so that one day she tried to trick him to his death. Instead, she fell into her own trap, as we shall see.

One day the Czar, who was his father, called Ivan and confided to him a terrible secret. "I hoped this day would never come," he said. "You must escape immediately. Years ago I had a dream in which I discovered that your stepsister would become a witch, and would try to kill you. Yesterday, before he died, the magician of the mountain told me that this would happen very soon."

At first Ivan protested, but his father convinced him. So, Ivan went to get his horse, and he rode away.

He rode for days, following the river that crossed the plains of his land. He rode until he saw the snowy mountains where the river sprang up, and here, in the thick pine forest, he finally stopped.

He built himself a house in the middle of the woods, and lived by hunting and fishing. Ivan tried to forget the terrible prophecy.

A year went by. One night, Ivan could not sleep so he went outside. He was walking along the banks of a stream, when suddenly in the moonlit water he saw the reflection of his stepsister's face.

Her eyes bewitched him and he knelt down over the stream, while a voice spoke to him: "My dear brother, come back to your castle. I am here waiting for you. Our father would like to see you. Why did you leave?" Then the vision disappeared. Ivan, frightened, stood up quickly. A shiver ran down his spine. He wondered, "Whom must I listen to?"

Suddenly he said to himself, "I must return, right away!"

The trip back to his castle was long. But Ivan continued on his way, following the far away sound of the bell tower. When he was told that the bells were ringing to announce the death of the Czar, Ivan rode even more quickly.

The walls of his city were finally in sight, when suddenly a strange procession came along. His sister stood in the middle of the road, followed by two squires who held an enormous scale, and by the hangman, who carried a large ax.

He heard his sister say, "I have been waiting for you! Your father is dead; he has left me this scroll on which is written his will. We must weigh ourselves on this scale, and whoever weighs less will succeed to the throne. The other must die!"

Ivan understood that his death was certain.

He weighed more than
his sister. She looked large,
but in fact, she had stuffed her
clothing to look heavier so Ivan would agree to her cruel test.
Destiny often follows a very strange path, however. The witch
had taken a seat on one of the plates, when suddenly there was
a loud noise: the bar broke, the plate tipped violently and she
fell to the ground.
The hangman, who had been given orders to kill the heavier
of the two, raised his ax overhead, and lowered it swiftly.
From that day on, Ivan was the Czar. He reigned for a long time,
and, as a symbol of justice, a scale was sewn into his family crest.

The Poplar and the Stream

Once upon a time . . . a woodcutter named Ivan lived in a forest in the north of Russia. A sturdy young man, he built himself a log cabin with his bare hands and when it was finished, he decided to look for a wife. His dream was to find a beautiful maiden, slender and fair, with blue eyes and creamy skin. On Sundays he roamed the distant villages looking for the girl of his dreams. But the girls he saw were not pretty enough. As it so happened, the path he took to work passed close to a pretty little house. Often, a sweet-faced girl would watch the woodcutter as he went by. He had unwittingly captured a maiden's heart: the young girl was named Natasha. She was shy, but her love for the woodcutter was so great that one day she stopped him on the path.

"I picked this basket of strawberries myself," she said. "Please eat them and think of me!"

"Well, she's not exactly ugly, but . . . ," said Ivan to himself as he stared at Natasha, who was blushing. "I don't like strawberries," he replied bluntly. "Thank you the same!" Tears sprang to Natasha's eyes as she watched him stride away. A few days later, the girl stopped Ivan again and held out a woolen jacket, saying, "It will be chilly tonight, but this will keep you warm. I made it myself."

But Ivan replied, "What makes you think that a man like me is afraid of the cold?"

This time, at Ivan's refusal two tears rolled down Natasha's cheeks and she fled sobbing into the house.

But she watched for the woodcutter. The next time, she held out a bottle and said, “You can’t refuse a juice that I pressed from all the fruits of the forest!” But Ivan said, “I don’t like juice,” and marched straight on. He realized he had been rude, and he turned around, but Natasha was gone. As he walked on, he said to himself, “She has gentle eyes . . . and she must be very kindhearted! Perhaps I should take at least one of her gifts —” At that moment, a beautiful lady appeared.

"Will you sing a song for me? I'm Rosalka, a woodland fairy!"
Ivan stood thunderstruck. "I'd sing for you for the rest of my life," he exclaimed, "if only I could . . . ," and he stretched out his hand to touch the fairy, but she floated out of reach. "Sing, then! Sing! Only the sound of your voice will send me to sleep!" So Ivan sang while the drowsy fairy urged him on. Cold and weary, his voice growing hoarse, the woodcutter sang until evening. But when night fell Rosalka, still awake, demanded, "If you love me, sing on! Sing!" As the woodcutter sang in a feeble voice, he thought, "I wish I had a jacket to keep me warm!" Suddenly he remembered Natasha. "What a fool I am!" he told himself, "I should have chosen her as my bride, not this woman who asks and gives nothing in return!" Ivan felt that only the gentle Natasha could fill his empty heart. He fled, but he heard a voice call, "You'll never see her again! Her tears have turned her into a stream!" It was dawn when Ivan knocked on Natasha's door. No one answered. The woodcutter saw that close by flowed a sparkling stream he had never noticed. Weeping, he plunged his face into the water. "Oh, Natasha, how could I have been so blind! I love you now!" Lifting his gaze, he silently prayed, "Let me stay beside her forever!"
Ivan was magically turned into a young poplar tree and the stream bathed its roots. Natasha, at last, had her beloved Ivan by her side.

The Prince and the Beggar

Once upon a time . . . near the mountains of Afghanistan, there was a small but wealthy town where caravans met on their return from India and China. The most beautiful building in the city belonged to

a merchant who had made a fortune in the spice trade.
The building was decorated with mosaics of every color, finely carved wooden doors, and columns and tiles of precious marble. Everyone who passed by stopped to admire its beauty. Next to the front door, however, there sat a beggar. No one ever gave him anything. In front of this palace, his poverty was even more evident.
One day a rich prince arrived in town, and, attracted by the magnificent beauty of the building, he stopped to admire it. When he saw the beggar he asked him, "Poor man, why are you in front of such a building?" The beggar responded, "Noble sir, to answer your question I would have to tell you a sad story, which I think you do not want to hear." "Come closer!" ordered the prince, who was curious. The beggar began his story and his eyes filled with tears. "I inherited this building from my father, who was the most successful merchant in all the country. When he died, I did not want to continue his profession; I preferred to spend my time at parties and banquets with my friends.

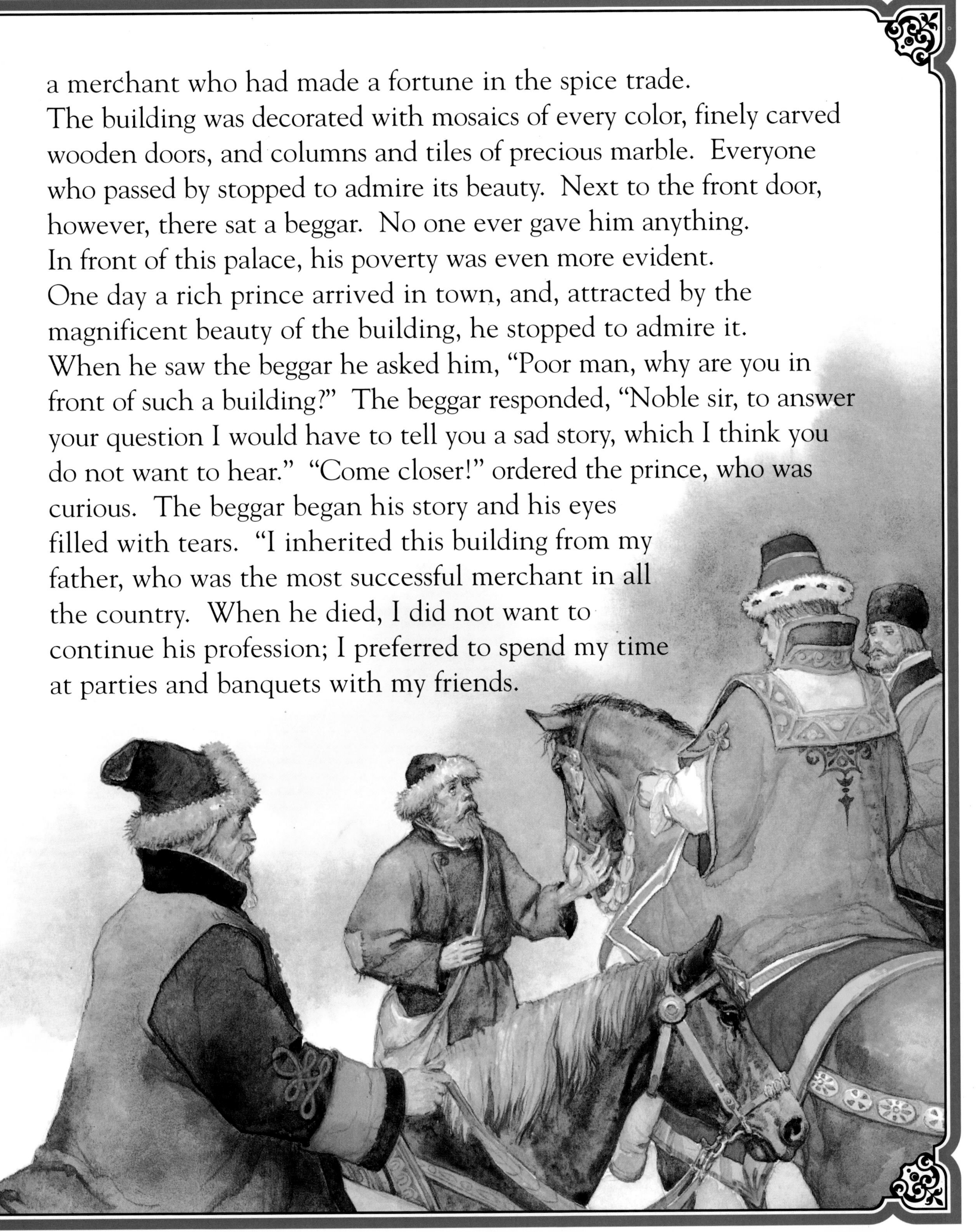

I lived in luxury, and I was very generous with the people around me. Then one day I realized I had spent everything. Full of debts, I lost this building, too."

Sadly, the beggar continued.

"By then I was poor, and I realized that I had also lost my friends. Now, what can I do but stand in front of what was once my home? Few are the passersby who will stop and give me something."

"That is a very sad story!" said the prince.

"If I could turn back time, I would be more careful and wise," said the beggar. "If only I had saved a little of the money I once had, today I would be a happy man."

"Wise words," responded the prince. "For your wisdom, I would like to give you something."

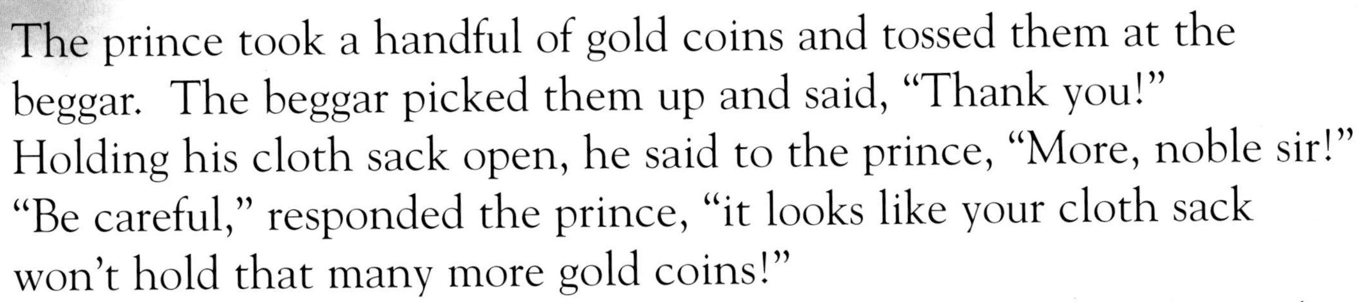

The prince took a handful of gold coins and tossed them at the beggar. The beggar picked them up and said, “Thank you!” Holding his cloth sack open, he said to the prince, “More, noble sir!”
“Be careful,” responded the prince, “it looks like your cloth sack won’t hold that many more gold coins!”
“The cloth is strong,” said the beggar, his eyes gleaming with greed. “Throw more coins, I beg you!”
A small crowd had gathered around them. The prince warned the beggar, “Your bag will break —”
Suddenly, the bag ripped and the coins rolled everywhere.
The crowd pounced on the coins, which immediately disappeared. The beggar burst into tears; once again he had lost everything because of his greed. The prince spurred his horse, shouting to his escort, “Let us go! Remember the lesson! Today you have seen a man who has learned nothing from life.”
As he crossed the square, the crowd applauded and shouted out, asking for more gold coins.

The Lake of the Golden Fish

Once upon a time . . . there was a lazy young man named Igor. He did not have a house, and spent all of his days sitting around. Even though he was sometimes very hungry, he had no intention of going to work. Every so often someone in the village would offer him a job, but he always turned it down. It was difficult for Igor to earn even a little something to at least put an end to his hunger. Even though everyone considered him to be lazy, no one could deny that in all of Russia there was not a man happier than Igor. He was always joyful and smiling. It gave him great pleasure to spend an entire day doing absolutely nothing.

When the weather was nice he slept in the woods at night, and when the sun was high during the day he rested in the shade of the trees. He would take a little something from the fields nearby, and did not have to worry about working to feed himself.

When the long, cold winters arrived, however, life became more difficult for Igor. He would knock on all the doors of the village until someone would take pity on him and offer him a hot meal and a place to sleep.

On one of the coldest nights that winter, Ivan was sleeping in a hayloft and found a bottle of vodka hidden in the hay. It was almost full. He took a few long drinks from the bottle, hoping that the liquor would warm him. It was very strong vodka, and he soon fell into a deep sleep. He began to dream a strange, wonderful dream.

He found himself on the shore of a lake filled
with goldfish, and he was fishing quite peacefully.
Soon something very extraordinary happened: as soon as
he pulled the fish out of the water they turned to gold!
The next morning Igor awoke with a terrible headache.
It took him a few minutes to realize that it had been a dream.
For the first time in his life he became very sad; he blamed the
vodka for its effect on him. But the following night, he did not
drink anything and yet he had the very same dream.

This continued for many more nights. The wonderful lake became an obsession. He was convinced that the lake existed; all he needed to do was to search for it. Then he would be rich.

As the spring arrived the snow melted, and the many lakes within the forest reappeared. Igor found himself a pole, some string, and a hook and he set off to go fishing. He soon became a very good fisherman. He knew exactly which bait the fish liked. But he was not able to catch any golden fish.

Some time passed and Igor, who once had been so happy, was always sad. One day, by chance, he decided to fish in the lake nearest to the village. He fished there all day.

The sun was setting when a fish finally took the bait. The fish leapt out of the water and, in that moment, the sun was shining its last rays and the entire surface of the lake turned golden. The fish, too, was captured in this strange light and looked just like gold to Igor. The young man shouted with joy and jumped to his feet. But Igor lost his balance and fell into the water.

The fish wriggled free. Igor was sad, but his enthusiasm returned, because he had discovered the lake with the golden fish.
From that day on he did not leave the banks of the lake. In the village Igor had told some people about the miraculous fish from his dream, and the word began to spread.

Many of the villagers traded provisions with Igor in exchange for fish. Some would even say, "When you catch a golden fish, put it aside for me!" Each one promised Igor something special in return for a golden fish. Some even said that he could sleep in their hayloft for the rest of his days.

Igor was convinced that sooner or later he would catch a golden fish, and so he was very kind to everyone, and everyone hoped that he would keep his promise.

Time went by and the exchanges continued. The villagers always had fresh fish, and Igor had never eaten so much in his life.

Everyone maintained the hope that the golden fish would bring wealth and happiness to the people of the village.

Word finally reached the Czar of Igor and his uncurable laziness.

It was also explained how happy Igor was, too.

But the Czar was very wise, and recognized something of himself in Igor, so he sent a messenger to the village.

"Igor, you are a very lucky man!" said the messenger. "I have instructions to send you to the court of the Czar of all of Russia! You will not have to do anything. Your only responsibility will be to stay with the Czar and keep him company without bothering him. For doing absolutely nothing you will also be paid very well!"

Igor listened. "Dear friend, maybe once upon a time I would have accepted. But I cannot. This lake is full of golden fish, waiting to be caught! How can I give up such wealth?"

The messenger left shaking his head. "What a strange fellow!"

Igor, not giving up on his dream, never left the banks of his lake.

Ever since, it has been known as "The Lake of the Golden Fish."

Alex the Hunter

Once upon a time . . . there was a hunter named Alex, who lived happily in a house on the edge of the wood with his wife. She was a beautiful young woman with lovely red hair, and her name was Natasha.

One day the Czar and his escort were hunting when they spied the lovely wife on the steps of her house. Struck by her beauty, the Czar said, "Who are you, and what is your name?"

"I am the wife of Alex, the hunter," responded Natasha with a smile.

The Czar let out a sigh and said, "Blessed is your husband who has you always near!" Then he turned his horse and rode off.

But the Czar continued to think of Natasha. He remembered her beautiful face and he was taken by the urge to see her again.

It seemed unjust to him that a powerful Czar as himself should remain alone. "I must do something," he said to himself. "I will not allow that such a beautiful woman makes only a simple hunter happy. Now that I have fallen in love with Natasha, I must have her at any cost."

He asked his minister for advice.

"Your Majesty, I agree that you must have Natasha at any cost. Get rid of Alex. Call him to the castle and give him an order, which he will not be able to refuse, to 'go I do not know where and bring me I do not know what.' "

The Czar was satisfied and he laughed. "As always, you are right. We will never see him again."

When Alex was told of the impossible mission, he returned home very sad. He hugged his wife, crying, and said, "How will I be able to obey such an absurd command? If I do not leave, I will certainly be sent to jail."

Natasha stroked his head and tried to console him. "I will ask my godmother, the fairy Malidussa, for help. I have never asked her for anything. She told me that if I ever needed her I should say her name and touch this pearl three times." As Malidussa was being invoked, the pearl fell to the ground and turned into a giant crystal ball, which rolled out the front door. When Alex went out after it, it continued to roll, inviting him to follow.

The sun was high in the sky when Alex, having followed the magical globe for hours, arrived at the top of a high mountain pass.

Tired, he stopped to rest as the ball kept turning in place. Then it began to go down a steep path.

Alex followed until he arrived in the valley below.
The ball continued to roll along into the middle of a field of daisies. Then it disappeared. Alex moved closer until he saw a hole in the ground. He threw a stone into the hole, but it made no noise.
He was frightened, but he thought of Natasha and his courage returned. He slid slowly into the dark hole. As he fell, he was turned about by a strong whirlwind. Suddenly there was a bright light and Alex was in front of a large castle.
The beautiful fairy standing in the doorway said,
"Finally! I am Malidussa. I know everything. But do not worry, I will help you and Natasha. Follow my advice very carefully."
Alex thanked the fairy.

"Take this magical mirror," she said, "and wait for the sun to set, then reflect the sun's last rays from this mirror onto your house. It will become a beautiful dwelling, and then will return to normal. Your house will remain modest, but you will be able to live there with your wife. Your happiness will create an illusion for all; they will think that they see a wonderful palace instead of a little house made of wood." Then the fairy gave him a golden horn. "You will have many enemies. If you are in danger, blow this horn and an enormous army will appear behind you. Even the most courageous will run!" The next day Alex arrived home. Natasha was waiting for him, and he told her all that had happened. The sun was setting and the hunter was just in time to reflect the last rays in the mirror. In a few minutes, the little wooden house had become a magnificent palace. When the sun set, all returned as it was.

But Alex and Natasha's happiness did not last long. The Czar, convinced that Alex was by now far away, came back to the forest to find Natasha. When he arrived, he was shocked by what he saw. He raced his horse back to his castle. There he put together an army of men and returned to the imaginary palace.

His army invaded the entire forest, and Natasha was frightened. She began to cry. "The Czar will destroy our house and kill us, too." Alex reassured her, telling her, "Don't be afraid! I will blow on the horn Malidussa gave me."

And suddenly there appeared an army of millions. As soon as the Czar and his men saw the incredible army, they threw down their arms and ran. From that day on, the Czar never set foot in the forest again, and Alex and Natasha lived happily ever after in their little wooden house in the forest.

Beautiful Basilia

Once upon a time . . . in a country village there were two poor farmers who had a daughter. She was obedient, and as beautiful as a flower. The young girl was named Basilia, and her parents loved her very much. When Basilia's mother died, her father remarried. His new wife was a widow, and she came to live with him, bringing along her daughter, Naga. Naga was ugly and spiteful. The beauty and goodness of Basilia made her stepmother very envious of her. Slowly, the new wife tried to convince her husband that Basilia's good face hid a very mean character.

One day she took what little her husband had saved and hid it under Basilia's mattress. Even though Basilia said she had not done anything, her father was convinced that she should no longer live with them. He took her into the forest to the old witch. The old woman lived in a wooden hut that rested on four large chicken's feet. When she saw the house and its owner Basilia was very frightened.

The witch promised the farmer that if Basilia were helpful around the house, she would at least have food to eat. When they were alone, the old witch said, “I will be back in a few hours, and by then you should have lit the fire in the stove, cleaned and straightened up the house, woven some cloth, and prepared the dinner!”
Basilia looked around, disheartened. “How will I ever do all of these chores in such a short time?” she asked herself.
Suddenly a little gray mouse jumped up on the table and said in a nice voice, “It’s been a long time since I’ve had a piece of cheese. Would you please give me some?” The girl was surprised.
“A talking mouse? But you seem very kind. I will try to help you.”

She found some cheese and gave it to the mouse. "Thank you," he said when he was done. "How can I make it up to you?"
Basilia sighed. "I will need a lot of help in cleaning up this house."
The mouse whistled, and from every corner of the house ran many little mice who went straight to work.
They lit the fire in the stove, cleaned the house, and once they had finished preparing the dinner, they disappeared. The last mouse to leave said, "Thank you for the cheese! It was for the King of Mice!"
When the witch got back she was very surprised. The girl had followed all of her orders.
The mice continued to help Basilia every day, and soon the house was sparkling and clean. The witch was pleased with her little helper, and started to care for Basilia very much.

In the meantime her father, full of remorse, decided to go and see his daughter. When the witch saw him she said, “Shame on you. You brought your daughter here so that I might punish her, and instead she is sweet and good and does not deserve to stay here as my servant. Take her with you, and here is a gift for her when she will marry.” The farmer was happy to be with his daughter again, and they returned home.

When the stepmother learned of the gift that the witch had given Basilia, she became very angry. The farmer tried to convince his wife that Basilia was sweet but the woman just envied her more.

She said to her husband, "Now you must take my daughter to the witch, too. She is better than Basilia and this way she will receive a gift as well."

The farmer was not able to say no, and a few days later he took Basilia's stepsister into the forest. The witch gave her the same orders, but as soon as Naga was alone, she sat down on a bench, angry that she had to do so much work.

Once again, the King of Mice asked for some cheese, but the only response from Naga was the threat of a broom, and he quickly escaped.

When the witch returned and saw that none of her orders had been carried out, she sent Naga to bed.

In the days that followed, the girl received only punishment. Soon, her mother came to visit her. "Ah, you are the mother of this horrible girl! Take back this good-for-nothing!" yelled the witch. The mother dared to ask, "And the gift for her dowry?"

"I'll give you a gift!" snarled the witch, as she chased mother and daughter with her broom.

They received their gifts, on their backs!

The Magician's Gifts

Once upon a time . . . near the border of China there was a kingdom that lay in a beautiful valley surrounded by tall mountains.

A river ran through the kingdom, and the land was very fertile. The people of the kingdom were mostly farmers and lived well. They had a lot of enemies, due to the fact that their land was so rich. The only access to the valley was through a narrow mountain pass, and soldiers were always stationed there. Led by a valorous warrior named Olaf, for years they had wielded off attacks from armies wanting to sack the kingdom. Olaf's courage was well-known throughout the kingdom. He had fought off enemy soldiers many times by himself. The king thought to keep Olaf in the kingdom by proposing his daughter in marriage. The princess was not beautiful, but Olaf accepted, thinking that one day he would become king. This marriage of convenience, however, left the princess unhappy and she spent many nights wide awake.

It was during one of these nights that the princess, hearing Olaf talk in his sleep, discovered the secret of his courage. As a child, Olaf had been adopted by the Magician of the Mountains who had given him a miraculous coat of silk. It made the wearer invincible. Olaf also spoke of another gift, but the princess did not pay any attention.

For some time the princess had been secretly in love with a frail courtier. She thought, "If he wears this coat, he will become a hero and I can marry him. My father will certainly have Olaf killed if he loses his courage." One night, after stealing the coat, the princess told her father that Olaf wanted to kill him and take over the kingdom. The king was furious and had Olaf arrested. Poor Olaf!

The princess told the courtier everything, and after he put the miraculous coat on he agreed to marry the princess.

In the meantime, Olaf was in prison. He knew that the end was near when he heard the guards say that the princess would soon remarry. From the lining of his pants, however, Olaf extracted a small ring. The Magician of the Mountains had given it to him, warning that it was "a miraculous ring, and when you put it on you can do whatever you wish, but only one time in your life." Olaf transformed himself into a dove, escaped, and flew back to the royal palace. He stopped in front of a young maid and said, "Do not be afraid. I am Olaf, the warrior. I need your help. If you trust me I will reward you!"

The girl agreed to help him. She knew that the courtier took the coat off when he went in the water. So, when the courtier went to the beach, she followed. When he took off the coat she picked it up,

and the dove flying overhead landed on the sand. Olaf turned back into himself. "Goodbye!" he said to his unfaithful wife. He jumped onto the courtier's horse and said, "We will find a new kingdom where my valor will be appreciated, and where we can live happily," and as the maid put her arms tightly around him, they rode away.

The House with the Green Roof

Once upon a time . . . there was a young warrior named Igor. He was strong and courageous, and had spent many years in the service of a prince. Many times he had risked dying in battle. After fighting for many years, Igor felt that he would like to live a more tranquil life. He dreamt of a roof overhead and a calm place

in which to spend his days, not going to battle any longer.
He wanted to find a wife, but for a soldier like Igor this was not easy. Once, many years before, he had saved the life of a wise old hermit, who many said was actually a magician. Igor decided to ask him for some advice. He climbed up the mountain and told the old man what he wanted to do. The old man put a hand on his shoulder and said, "If you want to find a wife who really will make you happy, you must pass a test of courage and generosity. If you accept, then I can help you." Igor, who was not lacking in courage, thanked the hermit, saying, "I am ready to take your advice."
The old man pointed to the highest mountain and said, "Beyond that peak you will find the Valley of the Blue Flowers. Near a stream you will find a white house with a green roof. There you will meet your bride. Remember: you must be courageous and generous!"
On the morning of the third day Igor finally saw the green roof of the house. He knocked on the door. No one answered, and so very slowly, he entered the house. But his hand moved quickly to his sword! In front of him was a horrible monster covered with scales!

Igor quickly recovered from the shock of finding such a repugnant being, instead of the woman of his dreams. He had already raised his sword when the beast, sad and frightened, covered its horrible face with its paws. The soldier did not know what to do. Finally, he made the only choice that seemed right to him.

"It is not this beast's fault that it is so ugly. I know many men who are much more dangerous than this little beast. It is not my enemy, so I will let it live."

With that he put his sword in its sheath and left.

Months went by. Igor traveled from village to village, hosted by people who knew him for his great valor. When he reached the city, even the prince invited him to the castle.

Igor led an active life and met many women, but not one was the right one for him. Igor wanted to feel his heart beating again, like it did the time he neared the house with the green roof.

One morning he decided: he would return to the Valley of the Blue Flowers. He rode for quite some time, until he saw the house with the green roof in the distance. Finally he had arrived! He got off his horse, and walked toward the house. As he did so, he heard the sound of a sweet voice singing. His heart began to beat like it had the first time. Igor pushed the front door open with his sword in hand, but he stopped in his tracks in wonder.

In front of him stood a beautiful young woman who was smiling at him. "Come in, Igor. I was expecting you! You probably wonder what has happened to the beast."
She went on. "I was that beast. Your generosity not only saved my life, it freed me from a horrible spell, and for this I shall always love you." In a few seconds, they were in each other's arms.
Beyond the snow-covered mountains, the old hermit smiled.
He had paid his debt of gratitude to Igor,
and had given him happiness for life.

Irina and the Spirit of the Forest

Once upon a time . . . in a small town on the edge of a large forest there lived an orphan named Irina. Everyone knew the poor young girl, and smiled at her whenever they met.

The young girl, who had a very vivid imagination, spent her days telling marvelous stories and making up very strange tales.
Every morning, before school began, her classmates would sit and listen to her. Irina would tell her stories, such as having seen a bear with the head of a bird, or the moon crying because it was so lonely. Or sometimes she told of a wolf who dressed up as an old woman to go to the marketplace.
Every day Irina told a different story. Irina's classmates enjoyed this beginning to their school day. As soon as the little girl began to speak everyone grew very quiet. When the teacher entered the room she found attentive faces watching Irina and listening to her stories. Sometimes the teacher even waited outside the door until Irina had finished her tale. Then she would enter the room clapping her hands and patting Irina, saying, "If you keep this up, one day you will become a wonderful writer!"

On some days, Irina would go directly to the town market after school and find a barrel to stand on, where she would start telling her stories. The passersby were drawn to her wonderful tales.
On her way home she would sing, and to anyone who asked where she had learned that song, she would reply, “The creek in the woods taught me this song!” Irina brought a note of happiness to all of the villagers wherever she went.
But in the village there was one person who was not fond of Irina. The blacksmith’s daughter, a mean and jealous girl, never spoke in school except to tell on one of her classmates. One day the girl came home and told her father that Irina was a liar and that she told amazing stories so that everyone would like her.

The blacksmith's daughter managed to convince him and the next day he went to the marketplace to hear Irina's stories for himself. Irina told the tale of a ferocious wolf that everyone was afraid of, but who had become Irina's friend and came to visit every evening. When Irina had finished and gone away, the blacksmith shouted, "Irina offends us with her outrageous tales! She thinks that we are all stupid and that we believe all of this nonsense!"

A woman turned to the blacksmith and said, "Let her be. She lives in a world all her own, but it is a happy world. She tells her stories not to impress us but because she actually believes them."

"Prove it!" said the blacksmith.

But the woman responded, "You do not know Irina as I do, and you have only heard one of her stories. You cannot judge her on just one story!" She urged the blacksmith, "Tonight we will go to Irina's house. Wait and see . . . you will be surprised!"

When darkness had fallen they went to Irina's house, creeping silently under her window. Irina sat alone in front of the fireplace, rocking on her chair as she talked to herself. The woman and the man tried to understand what she was saying.
". . . My friend the wolf, I wait for you every night! Why don't you come? Why do you leave me alone? In the daytime I hear the birds singing and have my friends to keep me company, but at night I am alone, and hear the hoot of the owl that frightens me. Everyone else has a mother and a father to protect them, but I do not."
The blacksmith was touched, and he turned to the woman, who had tears in her eyes. They realized that the poor young girl invented the stories so that she would not feel alone.
Suddenly the blacksmith had an idea. He saw a large hollow trunk and said, "I can carve a mask to look like a creature of the forest. When Irina sees me she will think that her stories have come true!"

Soon after, the girl heard a knock on the windowpane. Here was a new friend: the Spirit of the Forest! "Hello Irina," said the strange apparition, "In the forest we love your stories . . . tell one about me!" Then the spirit disappeared. The next day Irina told a new story about the Spirit of the Forest, saying that he had paid her a visit. After school, the blacksmith's daughter ran home and she said that Irina had made up yet another story. She was surprised when her father sternly said, "You must never speak badly of Irina. That story is true, and you must apologize to her." And so, on the same day, Irina found a new friend, and the blacksmith's daughter never told on anyone again.

The Starling's Song

Once upon a time . . . there was a starling who went every day to the goldfinch's nest for singing lessons. In a short time, the starling's song improved. One evening, all of the animals of the forest came to hear the starling sing. The branches of the trees were filled, and the badger even came out of his den. As soon as the starling began to sing, all of the animals felt happy. The song was beautiful.

Its sweet melody created a feeling of harmony among the animals.
The animals congratulated the starling, for his singing was very good. One night, under a full moon, a nightingale flew to a branch and began to sing. The song was sad but sweet. The fox was the first to hear the song. Some of the other animals heard the song, too, as did the starling. All of the animals said that the nightingale was the King of the Birds. The starling flew sadly back to his nest. How he would like to sing like the nightingale!
That night he dreamt he sang as well as the nightingale, and the following days he flew deep into the wood to practice the nightingale's song.
One day, he decided he was good and perhaps even better than the nightingale. When the animals were all assembled, he proudly began to sing. But the animals expected to hear the lively, happy notes of the starling's song. They did not recognize the sweet, sad notes of the nightingale; the sound was more like the squawk of a magpie.
Very quietly, the animals left one by one.
The frog finally said, "Enough!" and hopped away.
The next day, embarassed, the starling flew to the goldfinch's nest.
"What went wrong?" he asked sadly.
"You must not imitate the nightingale," the goldfinch replied.
"This will be a lesson for you. You must have faith in your own song and realize that it is what all of your friends enjoy hearing from you."
"What should I do now?" asked the starling.
"Sing . . . with happiness, which you do so well!" said the goldfinch.

Thanking him, the starling realized that each one is appreciated for what he or she does best.

The Daughter of the Forest

Once upon a time . . . there was a Czar who had three sons. When they were grown, the Czar decided it was time for them to get married. He took them to the walls of the kingdom and said, "Each one of you aim your bow in the direction you please beyond the wall. Where your arrow falls, you will find your wife." The three young men were surprised but they did as they were told. The oldest son aimed his arrow to the right and it fell in the garden of a wealthy merchant who had a daughter. The second son aimed to the left and his arrow fell in front of a window belonging to the daughter of a valiant general. Boris, the youngest son, also the best archer in the kingdom, hesitated. He finally raised his bow and pulled the arrow far back. Boris was sure that he had never shot an arrow further.

He began to look for his arrow, but he could not find it. He realized that it might have fallen in a very thick forest which no one ever dared to enter. He began to cut a path through the dense growth, but it was difficult. Finally, in a small clearing, he saw his arrow in the sand. Next to it, sitting by a brook was a beautiful girl dressed in rags. Boris was embarrassed. "Hello! What is your name?" he said. The young woman looked at him, and smiling, she said in a sweet voice sounds that he could not understand. Boris realized that she could understand him, but that she could not speak. The arrow reminded Boris of his promise to his father. The young woman was to become his wife. Boris was pleased despite the strange situation. If it was his destiny to marry this girl, then he would. He took her by the hand and said, "I am the prince, Boris, son of the Czar. I shot this arrow not long ago, knowing that where it landed I would find my wife. It is now our destiny to marry.

This makes me very happy . . . and you?"

With a joyful look in her eyes the young woman nodded.

Soon the weddings for the three brothers were celebrated. Then each of the young couples went to live in a different wing of the palace.

In the months that followed, while his brothers and their wives participated in the life of the court, Boris kept to himself. He was very much in love with his wife, but appeared with her in public as little as possible to save her the embarrassment of not being able to speak. The Czar regretted his odd method of having his sons choose their wives. He realized that Boris, in order to obey him, had married a woman that all ridiculed. The isolation in which his son lived made him very sad.

Some of the courtiers had even advised him to take his son's wife away from the palace. The Czar had not seen his daughter-in-law since the wedding day, until one afternoon he met her walking in the palace gardens. The young woman bowed deeply in front of him, and when she lifted her face, he saw that her eyes were full of tears. The old gentleman put out his hand, and he said, "Tomorrow evening you will be invited to the court ball, and we will open the dances together." That evening, everyone anxiously awaited the arrival of the princess. When she entered, everyone was speechless. The princess was splendid in her long gown of silver silk, and her blond hair dazzled with a tiara of pearls. The young woman bowed gracefully before the Czar.

The Czar said, "May I have this dance?"
"Certainly, your Majesty," she replied, "I am happy to be here."
An applause rose up.
The Czar hugged Boris, who said, "Every night I have been teaching my wife to speak; she has made great progress.
Perhaps it was your invitation that lifted her fear."
"Why was she unable to speak?" the father inquired.
"It is a sad story," said his son. "When she was little her father, a rich man, died suddenly. Her uncle, who was also her guardian, was interested in her riches, and he took her into the forest.
Squires brought food, and told her that if she left, her uncle would kill her. Years of solitude left her incapable of speech."
Soon the Czar announced that Boris would be his successor.
"I have seen his great wisdom in the love he has shown for his wife. To govern, the Czar must love the people;
I am certain he will be the best Czar for you!"

The End